Praise for "The Archae

"... pure fun, succeeds as a fast-paced archaeological adventure ..." – *Kirkus Reviews*

"It is Nancy Drew meets *The Goonies* with a twist ..."
– *Children's Literature*

"Oertel sets a brisk but not overly rushed pace early in the novel and never lets up, placing a series of increasingly complicated obstacles and mysteries in his protagonists' path until the cinematic conclusion ... a fun, engaging series for adventure and history buffs." – *Quill & Quire*

"**The Archaeolojesters** is great fun! The kids are resourceful but believably so, smart but not too smart ... a good, solid, well written adventure story that kids will really enjoy."
– *CM: Canadian Review of Materials*

"Preteens with a fondness for Indiana Jones will be entertained and educated ... Oertel keeps the action moving while sprinkling the text with fascinating details ..."
– *Montreal Review of Books*

The

ARCHAEOLOJESTERS

BOOK 2

PILLARS OF TIME

The Archaeolojesters
Text © 2010 Andreas Oertel

Published by Lobster Press™
1620 Sherbrooke Street West, Suites C & D
Montréal, Québec H3H 1C9
Tel. (514) 904-1100 • Fax (514) 904-1101 • www.lobsterpress.com

Publisher: Alison Fripp
Editor: Mahak Jain
Editorial Assistants: Katherine Mason & Stephanie Campbell
Proofreader: Camilia Kahrizi
Graphic Design & Production: Tammy Desnoyers
Production Assistant: Elena Blanco Moleón

 Canadian Heritage Patrimoine canadien   We acknowledge the financial support of the Government of Canada through the Canada Book Fund for our publishing activities.

Library and Archives Canada Cataloguing in Publication

Oertel, Andreas
     The archaeolojesters : pillars of time / Andreas Oertel.

(Archaeolojesters ; 2)
ISBN 978-1-897550-92-2

     I. Title. II. Title: Pillars of time. III. Series: Oertel, Andreas.
Archaeolojesters ; 2.

PS8629.E78A672 2010   jC813'.6   C2010-901320-4

Indiana Jones is a trademark of Lucasfilm Ltd.; Ping-Pong is a trademark of Parker Brothers Inc.

Printed and bound in Canada.

   BIO GAZ   Text is printed on 100% recycled post-consumer fibre.

For Diane

– Andreas Oertel

Acknowledgements

My sincere thanks to everyone at Lobster Press, especially my amazing, always patient editor, Mahak Jain.

BOOK **2**

The ARCHAEOLOJESTERS
PILLARS OF TIME

ANDREAS OERTEL

Lobster Press™

PROLOGUE

Anna was cold, and she was terrified.

A whole day had gone by since it had happened, though she still didn't know *what* had happened. She had been exploring the ruins with her father and Uncle Rudi – just as she had many times before – when something went wrong. But what had gone wrong?

"Come on, Anna, think," she said to herself. She crouched into a ball under a forest canopy, and tried to warm her bare legs by rubbing them.

Concentrate, Anna.

She recalled roaming among the site of the ancient ruins – the ruins most tourists to Egypt didn't bother with because they thought they were boring. And she remembered running past the giant toppled statue of Ramesses II and straight to the stones – the pillars. The place was always deserted and that's the way Anna liked it. Sure, the big pyramids at Giza, on the edge of Cairo, were amazing. But for a day of *real* exploring she loved the crumbling open-air museum at Mit Rahina. Again, she tried desperately to think. Her last memory was that of helping her father and uncle measure the center ...

A raven screamed somewhere in the distance, and the goose bumps already growing on her arms swelled into little anthills. Anna bit her lip to fight back the tears.

Where am I?

She knew her father, the renowned Dr. Bruno Wassler, had studied that site, especially the three stones, for years. But she had never really listened to his theories about those pillars. She just enjoyed being with her dad, the famous – some said crazy – archaeologist.

Anna looked to the clearing where the three stone pillars stood like sentinels. The stones here *appeared* to be the same as those at Mit Rahina, but she was definitely not in Egypt now. She was somewhere else.

Each circular stone column was roughly four feet in height, a foot and a half thick, and ten paces from its neighbor. The top of each pillar was capped by a wider, flared piece, so that the monuments resembled giant chess pieces. Hundreds of symbols and glyphs covered the surfaces. The three stones formed a triangle, and Anna had woken up in the middle of that triangle.

But *why*? And *how*?

The sun was beginning to climb above the tree line now and she groaned with pleasure as it warmed her skin. It had been a long, cold night. This place felt like – and even smelled like – a normal summer morning in the *Schwarzwald*, the Black Forest where she grew up in Germany.

But in her heart she knew she was someplace very different. How could she have been at the Mit Rahina ruins one minute, and then in a wilderness the next?

Anna now wished she had been more attentive to

her father and his lectures about the pillars. What was it he was always discussing with Uncle Rudi? Cosmic markers? Solar calendars? Timelines touching? Quantum something? It had made no sense when he told her these things, and it still made no sense. But now she realized she should have listened.

She felt guilty, because only yesterday on the drive from the hotel to the ruins he had seemed extra enthusiastic. "I have a new theory," he'd told Anna proudly, "that the symbols on the pillars are the key." But Anna was so excited to be back in Egypt, she barely registered what he'd said and never even bothered asking, "The key to what?"

How can I go home, if I don't even know where I am?

Thirsty again, Anna decided to walk back down to the river for a drink. She had discovered the river by accident when she first woke up and began wandering around, dazed and confused. The river was a five-minute walk to the east and moving about helped her think. Anna knew the turbid water would probably make her sick, but her mouth was so dry she didn't care.

Suddenly, something strange began to happen.

She looked around the clearing quickly, searching for whatever had alarmed her. The sun was now high overhead and the pillars cast no shadow on the grassy ground. Everything seemed normal. But the hairs on the back of Anna's neck stood up and she shuddered with trepidation. A low vibration began in the air above the stones and rapidly grew into a deafening thumping. She pressed her hands over her ears so hard she thought she would crush her own head.

THUMP. THUMP. THUMP.

She squinted through the pain toward the pillars in the distance. Anna desperately wanted to run away from the unbearable noise and those stupid stones – this had to have something to do with them. But she knew that whatever was going on now might be a clue to help her get back home.

So she stayed put.

The air over the stones continued to thump violently until it all ended with a final screech that sounded like the scrape of giant fingernails against a chalkboard. The abrupt silence and the relief from the painful pounding made a tear slide down Anna's cheek. She wiped it away with her shoulder and got up.

Wait!

There was a body lying in the clearing.

Anna hadn't seen the small shape in the center of the pillars until she stood, but she was sure she wasn't imagining it. To be certain, she rubbed her eyes vigorously and focused again. Yes, there was someone there. *That's exactly where I was when I landed here!* Anna thought.

Her heart beat a mad rhythm as she approached the still form. Who could it be? *Doesn't matter*, she quickly told herself. At least she wouldn't be alone anymore. Perhaps, between the two of them, they could figure out a way back to Mit Rahina.

A raven – maybe the same one she heard earlier – emitted a harsh shriek.

Anna froze twenty feet from the body. *Was that a warning cry?* She closed her eyes, alert to the sounds of the forest around her. She heard nothing, but then again, her ears were still ringing from all the thumping. But why was the raven screaming?

Anna moved forward cautiously. The body was that of a girl – a girl her age, perhaps twelve or thirteen. She was lying on her side with one arm under her blond ponytail.

Please don't be dead, Anna prayed.

The girl groaned and rolled onto her stomach.

KA-KAWWW! The raven shrieked again – louder this time.

Anna sensed someone might be approaching and felt a powerful urge to hide.

She knelt next to the girl's head. "Please wake up," she whispered urgently. She shook her gently and repeated the same thing in German. *"Bitte wach auf."*

The stranger groaned, but her eyes stayed shut.

KA-KAWWW!

Panic rose in Anna. "We have to hide," she warned.

She shook the girl again, and at the same time searched for cover. The girl opened her eyes, smiled weakly, and went back to sleep.

KA-KAWWW!

Anna hooked her elbows under the girl's arms

and attempted to drag her backward to the tree line. She made it five steps and collapsed, gasping for air. The girl's limp form was far too heavy for Anna to move alone.

The voice in her head implored her to run. *Go! Now!*

If she had more time, Anna could get them both to safety, but she didn't have a second to spare.

She had to hide now.

Anna left the girl amidst the pillars and sprinted for a cluster of uprooted trees. Diving over a fallen spruce, she curled into a ball and rolled to a stop. She was in the mossy depression of a giant root pad left behind when the wind knocked over the entire tree. Anna was safe for now, though her feeling of security couldn't mask the regret she felt at having to leave the girl behind. She grabbed a fistful of moss and squeezed it tight, frustrated that she was too weak to save her.

Shouts reached her from the far side of the meadow.

Anna pressed her face into the damp earth and tried to still her breathing. She didn't think they had seen her, but she couldn't be sure.

She didn't dare look up.

Waves of broken speech reached her from the area near the pillars. The dialect and tone were unfamiliar to Anna. She was good at languages and fluent in German, English, and Arabic, but she had heard nothing like this before.

Curiosity finally compelled her to chance a peek. A small gap between the fallen tree and the ground allowed Anna to see some of the area.

Eight men nervously formed a perimeter around the stone markers, while a ninth man examined the girl. A pillar obscured his face and he vanished from her sight quickly, but she saw that he was at least a foot taller than the other men and commanded respect. The men she could still see were clad in leathers and skins – they resembled the images of native North Americans that she had seen in books.

Her heart raced impossibly fast. She had been so worried about *where* she was, she had never even considered when she was. These were definitely not people from her time. *Had she somehow traveled to the past?*

Anna had failed to listen to everything her father tried to pass on to her, but she wouldn't make that mistake again. She concentrated on every detail, searching for clues that might help her rescue the other girl and get them both home again.

Five of the men held short bows and carried quivers on their backs with arrows. The other three were armed with fierce-looking spears. She examined the group and noticed they varied in age from older teenagers to senior citizens. The way the men were looking around and shifting about from foot to foot made Anna think they feared the stones.

Anna still couldn't see the tall man's face, but she saw him lift the unconscious girl and move her farther away from the columns. Anna thought, from the way the man was holding the girl, he wouldn't hurt her. But she couldn't take that chance, so she remained hidden. And even though she longed for the company of humans, Anna knew the answer to returning home – to her own time – was here at the pillars. She couldn't leave.

The pillars are the key. Her father had said so.

If another girl from her time could find her way here, her father could too. *I have to stay put – someone will find me.* She had to believe that.

Anna's thoughts were interrupted when one of the shorter men began arguing with the tall man carrying the girl. *Now what?* She noticed that the shorter man wore a necklace with a peculiar assortment of teeth, claws, and bones dangling from it. He must be a band chief or tribal ruler. The Chief barked at the man holding the girl. Some of the others became impatient and gathered around the tall man, as if in support.

It looked like the Chief wanted to leave the girl behind, but the taller man disagreed.

Finally, the tall man lowered the girl onto the grass and a stretcher was hastily rigged up using two of the longer spears and some pieces of leather.

As the party left the clearing, Anna whispered a quiet promise to the girl. "I won't abandon you a second time. I'll get you home too."

And there she waited, alone, as another cool night replaced the warmth of the sun ...

CHAPTER 1

Man, was it hot.

Sure, I expected it to be hotter in the desert than in Manitoba, Canada, but it still hit me like a hammer. Though, I may have just gotten used to lower temperatures because of the air-conditioned, twelve-hour flight from Canada to Egypt I had just taken.

No, it wasn't only that. When I got off the jet, it felt like I was breathing air from an oven. Really.

Eric and I followed Aubey, our chaperone for the trip, down the ladder and onto the asphalt. For a guy who was on his home turf again, he seemed pretty edgy this morning. "Stay close when we get inside the terminal," he said. "This is a busy airport."

We let Aubey move with the flow of disembarking passengers toward the terminal, and waited for Rachel to get off the plane and join us.

"I can't believe we're finally here," Rachel said. "In Egypt!" She stepped away from the crowd and began shoving her new electronic book reader into her backpack. She had downloaded every travel book available on Egypt before we left home and read for most of the flight.

"Hang onto this for me too." Eric tossed Rachel the thick instruction manual that accompanied his birthday present – a handheld GPS device.

Rachel shook her head. "Did you even crack it open?" She pushed the book into her pack, zipped it shut again, and headed toward the terminal.

Eric ignored her and stared at the dusty horizon. "Okay, so where are all the pyramids?"

The terminal looked like it was close by, but I realized that was only because it was so massive. The walk there was going to take a while. "I don't think they keep them at the airport," I said, laughing and following Rachel.

Eric didn't seem put off. He whooped and said, "This is going to be my best vacation ever!"

We caught up with Aubey and snaked our way through the ice-cold marble hallways of the airport into a vast baggage claim area. The four of us found a bench and waited for one of the shiny steel carousels to spit out our bags.

It was hard to imagine that only a few weeks ago we had fooled the world by planting a phony Egyptian tablet next to a river in our home town, Sultana. Our goal had been a noble one. That is, if playing a hoax on the world so your friends won't have to move can be considered noble.

In any case, our plan succeeded, and we managed to impress an international organization with our "ingenuity" and, I grimaced, our "cheeky audacity." I would have been happy with just the prize money, but the deal was we couldn't get the award unless we also took an "educational" trip to Egypt. It seemed that *some* of the Egyptologists hadn't appreciated our trick as much as the local media back home. And they thought we needed to be tuned in, I guess.

At first, Mrs. Summers – that's Eric and Rachel's mom – had been dead-set against us going to Egypt with a strange man, Aubey Benchouchou. My parents and Eric's mother invited Aubey over for supper, where they pestered him with a zillion questions about his organization and the proposed travel schedule. But it wasn't until Dad made a few phone calls to the police to have Aubey checked out – which I thought was going a *little* overboard – that they gave the trip their final blessings.

I had sighed with relief when at last I overheard Dad tell the moms that everything would be just fine. "Let the kids go," he said. "This will be an adventure they'll never forget."

He had that right.

Eric jarred me back to the present with a poke in the ribs. "I think that's Aubey's bag."

Aubey had seen it too. He jumped up from his seat and stormed off to retrieve his luggage. We watched as a stranger flipped the ID tag on Aubey's bag before he could get to it. Aubey glared at the man and he cowered away to continue searching for his own suitcase.

Eric leaned over and whispered, "Why is he mad all the time?"

"He's been acting funny," Rachel said, "ever since we touched down."

"Maybe he's still upset he was forced to babysit us," Eric suggested.

Aubey quickly returned with his bag and shifted from foot to foot, waiting for us to spot our packs. His mouth was closed tight and he had a determined set to his jaw.

Eric reached out and poked Aubey to get his attention. "Do you know where the can is?" Eric asked.

Aubey stared at Eric. "The what?"

"The john. The biffy." Eric laughed. "The *restrooms* – where are they? I have to go."

Aubey froze. "Can't it wait until we get to the hotel?"

"Okay," Eric said, confused. "I suppose I can –"

"What's the big deal, Aubey?" I asked. "Do we need to get somewhere in a hurry?"

Aubey searched the crowd and laughed, but it sounded forced. "No ... well, it's a busy place. That's all. You might get lost."

Eric shook his head in disbelief.

Rachel joined in and supported our chaperone. "Just hold it until we get to the hotel," she told her brother. "Stop being a nuisance."

Eric snorted. "This is going to be a pretty lame trip if we can't even pee when we have to pee."

Aubey's cell phone suddenly chirped – for the third time since we landed. He scowled at the caller ID and pushed a button to silence the ring. Aubey had answered the first call while we were still on the plane, waiting for the ladder truck to pull up. The conversation seemed to start off civil, but then Aubey's face had turned beet red and the vein on his temple pulsed and twitched for so long I thought it would burst. In the end, I think he just hung up on the caller. Maybe someone was trying to sell him something and he was tired of being pestered.

I watched Aubey as he *again* scanned the faces of the people around us – like he was looking for someone. When he finished his search, he passed his phone to Eric and said, "You should call your mother and tell her we've arrived."

Eric frowned. "But we just got here. We haven't even been away twenty-four hours yet!"

Aubey sighed. "I know," he admitted, "but I promised your parents that we would call as soon as we landed safely. And we have now landed safely."

Eric shook his head at the craziness of adults and called home. When he finished telling his mom the plane *hadn't* crashed, he passed the phone to me.

Dad answered after only two rings and I told him we had a great flight and everything was fine. The line crackled and I heard Mom's voice on the extension phone. She said pretty much the same thing Dad had said: "Be careful, have fun, eat well, listen to Aubey, stay out of trouble, and ... and be careful."

I passed the phone back to Aubey, and at the same time he slipped me another identical phone. "This is for all of you, Cody," he said. "It's good for you to have a cell phone just in case ... in case of an emergency." He showed me how to use the basic features and how to access the numbers in the phone's memory. "And please don't turn the power off. It has a built-in tracking system, so I can find your phone using my phone." He punched a few buttons on his phone and a map appeared on the display. Two overlapping dots flashed on the screen, superimposed on a map of Cairo.

I took the phone, but gave him a strange look: it was almost like he was *expecting* us to get in trouble. "What about a charger," I asked, "for the battery?"

Aubey nodded. "The battery is powerful and will last for ten days when the phone is asleep – on stand-by. You won't need a charger. Just don't make silly phone calls."

I laughed. "Come on. Is Egypt really this dangerous?"

Aubey's face became grave. "I have been entrusted with an important task – your safety. And I take that assignment very seriously."

"Okay, okay," I said. "I guess we just aren't used to all these precautions in Sultana."

Aubey must have realized he was freaking me out a bit, so he changed the subject. He reached inside his jacket and handed us each a single sheet of paper. "This," he said proudly, "is the travel itinerary for your stay in Egypt."

Our parents had asked lots of questions about the sites we'd be seeing, but we couldn't figure out what most of the names meant. This was the first time we'd seen the list of places we would be visiting, and the times and dates Aubey would take us there.

Eric looked up from his paper. "Are any of these things amusement parks or waterslides?"

Aubey opened his mouth but didn't answer. Maybe he thought Eric was kidding.

"Don't be an idiot," Rachel said. "We didn't travel all the way to Egypt to ride roller coasters."

"I know. I'm just thinking that after we go to –" Eric looked at the schedule "– *The Museum of Islamic Arts*, maybe we could ride bumper cars or do something fun. What's wrong with that?"

This time Rachel was speechless.

"Do we have to do stuff in this order?" I asked.

"Yeah. Can we go see the King Tut stuff first?" Eric said. "That might be cool."

Aubey ran his fingers through his thick black hair, and I thought I heard him groan. "We will see these sites," he said slowly, "in the order indicated." He tapped the agenda Eric was holding. "*That* is what I told your parents."

"But they're not here," Eric objected. "There's nothing wrong with *tweaking* the schedule a bit."

Aubey sighed. "There will be no 'tweaking.'"

"Yeah," Rachel repeated with a grin, "no tweaking."

My bag popped out next and I stowed my cell phone – sorry, Aubey's cell phone – in one of the outside pockets. When we all had our luggage, we merged into a new lineup for customs. It went pretty smoothly, even though Aubey was behaving like someone who was guilty of everything. He sure wasn't acting like the polished, worldly explorer we thought he was when we first met him.

We left the comfortable modern airport and walked back into the mid-morning heat.

"This way, children." Aubey herded us past hundreds of waiting taxis. Each cabbie did his best to coax us into his car, but Aubey ignored their Arabic banter. He walked all the way to the far side of the terminal, and then to the very end of the taxi pickup area.

Finally, he stopped and announced, "The company car will pick us up here. But stay close to me, and don't wander off!"

Eric rolled his eyes. He threw his bag in front of a bench and sat down to wait. "I hope they send a sleek black limo for us – one with a mini-kitchen."

I pulled out my digital camera – an early birthday present – and began snapping pictures. "Hey Aubey," I said. "Take a picture of the three of us."

His eyes darted back and forth, searching through the throng of people and cars behind us. He took my camera and hurriedly clicked a few photos of us huddled together on the bench, grinning like dolphins. We were going to have a good time, even if our chaperone wasn't. If he wanted to be a party-pooper, that was his problem.

Eric stayed slouched on the bench but Rachel and I were too excited to sit still. We jumped up as soon as

Aubey gave me back my camera, and I took some more pictures of Rachel hamming it up. That was when she surprised me with a hug. "Thanks, Cody," she said. "Thanks for making that plaque, thanks for coming to Egypt, and thanks for *not* letting us move."

"OH, GROSS!" Eric yelled, pretending to gag. "Come on, you guys. I have an empty stomach and I'm already queasy."

If I was hot before, waiting under the Egyptian sun, I was even hotter now. I felt my face burn from embarrassment and mumbled, "No problem."

But that was when our problem started.

Aubey, who had his eyes on the road, spun around when Eric yelled. At the same time, a cab pulled up to the curb and two men wearing baseball caps approached him from behind. Long shadows cloaked their faces, so I couldn't really see what they looked like. The larger man tossed our bags in the trunk using hands the size of baseball gloves, while the other cabbie stayed glued to Aubey, just behind his right shoulder.

Eric stood up and kicked his bag. "Crud!" he said. "I guess our limo ride got canceled, right?"

The smaller cabbie said something to Aubey, who nodded with short, quick jerks of his head.

Aubey had been in a bad mood all morning, but he looked even more tense now. "Aubey? Is everything okay?" I moved toward him.

I saw the smaller cabbie's lips move again. Aubey gave me a tight smile and nodded. I hesitated, and then followed Eric toward the car.

"That just figures," he griped, handing one last bag to the cabbie. "I sure hope they have food at the hotel."

The trunk slammed shut and two seconds later the bigger cabbie hustled us into the rear seat. "*Besora'a.* Hurry," he said.

I was the last person to climb into the cab before it pulled away. It all happened so fast, I barely registered that Aubey *wasn't* in the car with us. When I turned to look out the rear window, I saw him chasing the cab and screaming at the top of his lungs. I couldn't believe my eyes. I wasn't sure what was going on, but it didn't look good.

Eric and Rachel were still preoccupied with our travel itinerary. They hadn't even noticed what just happened until they heard the shrieking behind us.

"Hey," Rachel said, realizing we were on the move. "Isn't Aubey coming with us?"

She whirled around and we both watched as Aubey tried to catch our rapidly accelerating cab. His legs powered him easily for three hundred feet, but once we cleared the congestion of honking cabs, his grimacing face disappeared amid a sea of vehicles.

"What's happening?" Rachel dropped the map on the floor of the car.

I almost had to scream to be heard above the noise of wind and traffic mayhem. I turned to my two best friends. "I think we've just been kidnapped," I said.

CHAPTER 2

Eric was staring wide-eyed out the back window. When he heard what I said, though, his face softened and he laughed. "No way! Relax. Aubey's just trying to get back at us for tricking him. And back at me for clobbering him."

"I'm not so sure," I said. "Now that I think about it, he had a funny look on his face when these guys snuck up on him. I think the guy driving, the shorter one, may have had a gun pressed against his back."

"I think I'm going to be sick," Rachel said. She began to breathe in and out rapidly. "This is serious."

"Well, of course it *looks* serious," Eric said. "He *knows* we're not going to fall for a stupid little trick. He's going all out to teach us a lesson. And, hey, Cody – that's why he gave you his phone, remember? He's trying to spook us!"

Rachel looked across Eric, at me. "What do you think?" she asked.

I shrugged. "I suppose it's possible, though kind of extreme."

"Yeah, it's extreme," Eric said. "But remember, I bashed him on the head with a shovel and almost killed him. Now *that* was extreme!"

Rachel seemed to calm down a bit when she

considered that. "It could explain why Aubey was acting so bizarre this morning," she said. "He may have been *pretending* that we were in danger, because he *wanted* us to be afraid. But I still think I'd feel better if we tried to call him."

"Good thinking ..." I said. "Oh rats! The phone's in my bag, which is in the trunk of the car."

Rachel started to look panicky again.

"Eric's probably right," I said, trying to calm both her and me down. "These guys probably work for Aubey's company. Remember they wanted to teach us a lesson? Maybe *this* is what they actually meant."

"Exactly! Maybe our encounter with these two is the start of the *real* itinerary," Eric said, delighted by all the action. A thick plastic shield separated the back of the cab from the front, but Eric tapped the window behind each man's head. "I mean, look at them. Do they look like criminals to you?"

Both men reacted to the rap on the divider and briefly twisted their heads sideways. They had removed their caps, and I saw they were both sweating up a storm. Their heads were shiny with perspiration, even though the front windows of the car were rolled down, allowing plenty of stinky, smoggy air in. Neither man looked Egyptian. In fact, they looked kind of like ...

"Oh my gosh," Rachel said. "These are the guys who tried to steal our fake tablet back in Sultana!"

"The Germans?" Eric leaned forward and pressed his head against the shield, trying to look at their faces from various angles.

Big Hands flipped open a plastic window cut into the security shield. "Please sit back down," he said in an unmistakable German accent. His giant body was cramped against the passenger door so that the driver, half his size, could reach the controls. He closed the opening again, sealing us in the rear.

"Now I'm really confused," Rachel said, her voice rising again in alarm. "Does this mean Aubey lied to us? Are the Germans in on his prank?"

"Or maybe," I suggested, "we really *have* been kidnapped."

The car slowed at a traffic circle and I tested the door handle. It didn't budge. "Well," I said, "we won't be escaping at the next stop sign. They've locked us in."

Rachel played with the button by her arm and tried to roll down the slightly-open window all the way. "They locked the windows too," she groaned. "We gotta get away from these guys," I said. "Let's try and get someone's attention."

"HELLLLLP!" Rachel screamed through the three-inch gap at the top of her window. She smacked the tinted glass with her hands as we passed a tour bus.

Both men in the front jumped, startled by Rachel's yell. The driver fumbled with his controls, quickly rolling up all the windows. The inside of the car suddenly became very quiet. He hit another switch on the dashboard and we instantly felt the cool breeze of the air conditioner.

"WE'RE BEING KIDNAPPED!" I hollered. The sealed windows would probably silence our screams to the outside world, but I continued hitting the glass and yelling anyway – I had to try something.

Eric slumped in his seat, dejected that we had abandoned his prank theory. He began kicking the back of the bench seat in front of him as hard as he could. The car swayed a little before the driver regained control.

The man behind the wheel finally got tired of being kicked in the kidneys. Keeping his eyes on the road, he opened the hole in the plastic. "You are *not* being kidnapped. We need your help. Urgently." To emphasize the urgency he looked at his wristwatch.

Eric stopped hoofing the seat and yelled, "Help with what?"

The two men shot nervous glances at each other before the driver spoke again. "We will show you soon. Could I see your passports please?"

Rachel folded her arms across her chest. "No way!"

"Forget it!" I said.

"First throw all your guns out the window," Eric said, "and then I'll show you my passport." Eric winked at me, obviously pleased with his negotiating skills.

"What?!" The driver seemed horrified at the idea of a firearm. "We have no guns."

"Yeah, right," Eric yelled through the plastic hole. "Then what did you press into Aubey's back?"

"Ohhh," the man behind the wheel said. He reached into his shirt pocket and pulled out some kind of handheld electronic device. It looked like a thick felt-tipped marker. "I told him this was a pistol, and he believed me."

"HA!" Eric yelled triumphantly. "So then you admit you're kidnapping us?"

Big Hands grew tired of Eric's interrogation. "Please believe us when we tell you that you are *not* being kidnapped. We only need your help for a few hours. Now may I see your passport?"

Eric, who always had to do things his own way, tossed his passport through the window at the driver. "Come on, you guys," he pleaded to Rachel and me. "This could still be part of Aubey's prank. Now that these guys are talking to us we might be able to figure out what Aubey has in mind. And then, maybe we can outfox him and play an even better joke on him. This could be so cool."

The driver flipped open Eric's passport and glanced at the photo page. He passed it to Big Hands and said, "*Gut*. Good."

Big Hands slipped it through the plastic back to Eric and said, "May I see yours now?"

Rachel and I hesitated. Eric had gotten his passport back right away – maybe they just wanted to make sure they had pulled their prank on the right kids – or kidnapped the right kids. Like I said, I still wasn't sure what was actually going on yet.

Rachel and I handed over our passports. They received even less attention than Eric's had and were quickly returned.

"So where's your evil lair?" Eric asked, grinning. "Where are you taking us? Are you going to rough us up a bit?"

Neither man responded: they were too busy looking at their watches and staring up at the sky. Maybe they thought police helicopters were following us.

Eric discreetly fished his GPS from Rachel's bag and turned it on. He placed the handheld tracking device behind the back of the seat, so that our captors couldn't see it, but we could. I imagined all the satellites way up in the sky looking for Eric's unit. Suddenly, the screen came to life with all kinds of information: direction, altitude, speed, etc.

"Check this out," Eric whispered. He pressed a few more buttons and showed us a screen with a map of Cairo. A tiny triangle flashed and moved down the crowded highway on the display, away from the airport. "That's us," Eric said, proudly tapping the triangle. "We're heading south on the Cairo Aswan Road."

Rachel leaned forward and spoke through the hole in the plastic. "At least tell us where we're going."

The driver sighed. "Okay. My name is Dr. Bruno Wassler," he said, sounding oddly guilty. "And this is my brother –"

"– Please call me Rudi," Big Hands said.

Dr. Wassler continued, "We are taking you to Memphis – to Mit Rahina. It's only twenty minutes from here. Everything will make sense to you when we're there. It's complicated – and you have to *see* the site to understand."

Eric looked at the screen on his GPS and nodded. "Yup, that's what we are headed toward." He tapped a dot on the display. "He's telling the truth about where we're going, anyway."

I picked up Eric's travel itinerary from the floor of the car. *Mit Rahina. Mit Rahina.* I searched down the schedule. *There it is!* "I knew that sounded familiar," I whispered. "That place is on our itinerary." I poked the name with my finger and showed my friends.

Rudi looked up at the sun through the windshield. The sun was pretty much where it was when he had last looked – only five minutes ago – but he frowned at it, like he was annoyed. "We *need* your help," Rudi said through the still-open window, "and we have to hurry – before it's too late."

"Look," I said. "You guys keep telling us that you need our help, but you haven't told us with *what*?"

Dr. Wassler and Rudi said nothing.

"And why did you try and steal our fake tablet back in Canada?" I asked.

Rudi didn't turn to look at us, but he tilted his head slightly so we could hear him through the window. "We didn't know that you made it when we tried to steal it."

"So you admit that you wanted to steal it?" Rachel asked.

"Yes." Rudi sighed. "But not for the reasons you may think."

Eric continued to monitor our location on his GPS. "Yeah, sure," he said. "Now just tell us once-and-for-all if this is a *fake* kidnapping or a *real* kidnapping. You're scaring my sister and upsetting her."

Rachel gave Eric an annoyed look and opened her mouth to protest. But Eric's words struck a nerve with both men, who exchanged ashamed glances. Eric elbowed Rachel and she closed her mouth, but not before shooting him a second nasty look.

Dr. Wassler tried to say something, but it looked like he didn't know where to begin. Finally, he took a deep breath and said, "My daughter, Anna ..." He blinked away a few tears and then started again. "My daughter, Anna, disappeared yesterday at the ancient ruins of Mit Rahina. We think you may be able to help find her."

Eric shook his head in confusion. "So *she* got kidnapped?"

Rudi closed his eyes, groaned, and pinched the bridge of his nose. "No one has been kidnapped!" he whined.

"Maybe she ran away," I offered.

"No!" Rudi barked. "She would never run away."

Rachel pulled out her e-book reader and turned it on. "If she disappeared, but *wasn't* taken by anyone, then she must be at those ruins."

"Perhaps," Dr. Wassler said, "but she isn't there."

"Then *I* think you guys need the local police," I said, "not three kids from Canada who have never even been to Egypt."

"Please be patient," Rudi begged. "It will all become clear at the ruins. If you then still wish to leave, we will take you back to Cairo – and Aubey – immediately."

At the mention of Aubey, I remembered something. "Hey," I whispered to my friends, "Aubey will be able to follow us using the phone."

"Huh?" Rachel said, leaning over her brother. "How?"

"He told me that the cell phone I have has a GPS tracking device built in. Even if these guys are *real* kidnappers, Aubey will definitely be able to find us."

"You don't think they're real either?" Eric asked, pleased to have an ally.

"I'm still not sure," I said. "Maybe they *are* part of his prank ... but what if this isn't a prank?"

We sat back and nervously watched houses made of concrete, brick, and stone pass by. It was an interesting drive, but I wouldn't say it was pretty. Most of Cairo seemed loud, busy, and kind of dirty, in the way big cities usually are. It wasn't at all like the peace and quiet of Sultana. The trip didn't really get scenic until we crossed the Nile and left Cairo. I was desperate to take my mind off whatever was happening, so I took out my camera and snapped pictures of the many orchards and farms along the floodplain.

That was when I thought of a test. I told Rudi to smile and then quickly took his picture through the plastic shield. He didn't smile, but he didn't seem to care that I had taken his picture. I thought that was a good thing. On TV, the bad guys never want their pictures taken. I clicked a picture of the side of Dr. Wassler's head and got the same result – no reaction.

When Rachel saw what I was doing, she snapped her fingers, and then opened the thousand-page encyclopedia that was in her e-book. She did a quick search, and I could tell she'd found what she was looking for when she slumped back in her seat with a satisfied smile. She passed her e-book to Eric, and I leaned over to take a look. We both read the short biography that accompanied the photograph of Dr. Wassler:

Dr. Bruno Wassler

Bruno Wassler received his Masters in Archaeoastronomy from the University of Bern, Switzerland, and obtained his Doctorate in Astrochronology from Oxford University, England.

Dr. Wassler is considered to be a leader in the fields of Petroforms and Petroglyphs, Cultural Astronomy, and Solstitial Alignments. He currently lectures at Cambridge University.

Eric shrugged and passed the e-book reader back to Rachel. "I have no idea what any of that means," he said. "But at least we know he's really who he says he is."

Rudi looked over his shoulder and through the

divider at the e-book reader, and then said something in German to Dr. Wassler. Dr. Wassler rolled his eyes at his brother, looked at his wristwatch, and kept weaving through the traffic. I didn't think they could hear us on the other side of the plastic divider, but we still tried to keep our voices down.

"Look him up now." I said, pointing at the back of Rudi's giant head.

Rachel nodded and tapped the touchscreen keyboard with her fingers. Two minutes later Eric and I were staring at a photo of Rudi and reading his bio. Here's what it said:

Rudi Wassler

Rudi Wassler is currently head researcher in the Physics Department at Cambridge, where he conducts experiments with quantum particles. A strong believer in time travel, Wassler has often been criticized by his academic peers for his unconventional ideas.

Wassler has written many papers on singularities, quantum tunneling, and traversable wormholes. He and his brother, Dr. Bruno Wassler, are founders of the controversial Ebenezer Project.

I poked the last two words on the screen with my finger. "The *Ebenezer Project*? That's a silly name for a project."

"I think these guys are actually pretty smart – not just common thieves – so now I really don't understand why they were trying to steal our plaque," Rachel said, taking back the digital tablet.

Eric pulled out a packet of cookies from his pocket and began eating. "If they're so brilliant," Eric said between chews, "why did they grab us? We're useless to them."

The cab slowed down when we passed through a construction area. The sudden drop in road noise from outside allowed Dr. Wassler to hear Eric's comment. "You are far from useless, young man," he said, looking at us in the rearview mirror. "In fact, you may be our *only* chance to get Anna back."

CHAPTER 3

"You guys are both some kind of genius academics," Eric scoffed, "but *you* need *our* help? Yeah, right. More likely, you and Aubey are up to something."

Both men ignored him. "We are here," Rudi said, sounding relieved.

The car pulled into a huge gravel parking lot about a mile from the highway. The lot was mostly empty except for a tour bus and some food-vendor carts. A group of tourists were boarding the bus, and the local street vendors were doing their best to sell them grub.

"This could be our chance to escape," I said. "Be ready for anything."

Rachel and Eric both nodded, but I could tell by the look on Eric's face that he still didn't think we had anything to escape from.

Dr. Wassler parked the car as far away from the bus and the vendors as he could. Rudi got out and opened our doors. We piled out quickly. The food sellers glanced our way, but must have thought it wasn't worth the hike over to pester us. One vendor gave us a hearty yell of *"Aish baladi?"* and then *"Kofta?"* But Rudi waved him off before he had a chance to harangue us further.

Eric looked longingly at the food carts near the tour

bus. "Whatever they're selling, it sure smells good. Maybe we could stop to eat?"

"Do you like pita bread and spicy minced lamb?" Rudi asked, clearly expecting him to be turned off.

But there was no deterring Eric. "Hmmm," he said, staring longingly at the food sellers. I swear I heard his stomach growl.

The three of us stood around the car and watched Dr. Wassler search for his rucksack. It took a few minutes for him to get organized because our luggage was in the way. Rudi opened a small cooler and passed us each a bottle of water. "It will be hot soon," was all he said.

"It's hot now," Eric replied. He twisted off the plastic cap and sucked down half the bottle. I suppose the cookies he ate in the car had made him even thirstier.

I stepped back and observed our kidnappers as they messed around with the luggage in the trunk. They were both probably the same age as Mom and Dad – in their forties – and they did seem brother-like in appearance. Each man had dark brown hair, and brown eyes, and wore glasses. Except Rudi looked more like an Olympic wrestler than a scientist – he was enormous.

Dr. Bruno Wassler, on the other hand, looked like a professor, or what I thought a professor looked like. He was smaller and shorter than his brother, and I could easily imagine him lecturing students about whatever crazy stuff he was an expert in.

I broke the seal of the water bottle, took a sip, and checked out the surrounding open-air museum – that's what Rachel said it was. It was hard to tell what attracted people. The edge of the parking lot was lined with towering sycamore trees and paths that went off in many directions. I saw lots of signs and touristy-looking arrows, pointing every which way, but there were certainly no pyramids in sight – and still no Aubey.

"Please follow me," Dr. Wassler instructed. "It's a fifteen-minute walk from here."

"Look," I said, "we need a couple of minutes. We want to talk – alone." I knew it was a long shot, making requests to our kidnappers, but it was worth a try.

The men looked at each other for a few anxious seconds. Then Rudi said, "Okay. That's fine. But please remember, we don't have much time left, and we *need* your help."

"Yeah, yeah," Eric said, "so you've said."

Dr. Wassler and Rudi walked to the trailhead and waited for us by a sign marked *The Walk of Sekhmet*. They were too far away to eavesdrop, but close enough that they could keep an eye on us.

Rachel picked up her backpack. "Should we make a run for it?" she asked.

"We could," I said, "but ..."

"Come on you guys," Eric pleaded. "Let's just see what they want to show us. I mean, do you *really* think these guys are kidnappers? There's no way! And, even if we did take off, where would we go? All our stuff –

including the phone, the only way Aubey can find us – is still locked in the trunk."

"I suppose we could see what's down the trail," I said. "They do seem to be desperate for our help."

Rachel looked north toward Cairo.

"Come on, Rachel, please," Eric begged. "Aubey wouldn't let anything bad happen to us. He's probably hiding in the trees somewhere right now, waiting to see if we'll chicken out or not."

Rachel scrunched up her face. "But what if they *are* kidnappers? What then?"

"If you really, truly believe that, we can all stand here and scream for help at the top of our lungs," Eric said. "Then the cops will come, drive us back to the airport, and we'll be on the next plane to Canada. Now what kind of holiday would that be?"

Rachel only frowned in response.

"We *are* at a museum – a huge public place," I added. "I can't see any harm in seeing whatever they want to show us. In an hour this place will be swarming with tourists. Kidnappers don't take kidnappees – or whatever we're called – to museums."

Rachel laughed. "Yeah ... I suppose that's true. And they did let us have time to chat alone. Kidnappers wouldn't do that ..."

"And I still have questions for these guys," Eric said. "I want to know *why* they flew to Manitoba to steal our phony plaque."

"Okay, okay. But if something terrible happens, I

will say 'I told you so.'"

"I expect no less." Eric rolled his eyes. "But what could possibly happen? We're at a museum. And remember, this place *is* on the itinerary the Egyptologists planned for us."

So that settled it. We walked to where the scientists were waiting and then followed them down a gravel path that wound around trees, through collapsed ruins, and between all sorts of interesting statues and pillars. But Dr. Wassler and Rudi never slowed down long enough for us to get a good look at any of them.

After ten minutes of hurried hiking, we finally stopped to take a break. Rachel rested next to a stone statue of a car-sized dog and drank from her water bottle. She pulled my camera out of her backpack. "Here," she said, passing me the camera. "Take a picture of me next to this lion. We might as well have fun if we're here."

"Yeah," I said, "Oh, and you're right. It *is* a lion. I was sure it was a dog." I took a picture of a sign that said *The Lion of Nubia* in six different languages, and then snapped a few photos of Rachel standing in front of the dog that was supposed to be a lion.

Rudi cut our break short when he ran back down the trail to fetch us. "Please, Cody. Please, Rachel. We must hurry. It's almost time."

I got tired of asking, "Time for what?", so I didn't. Every time I tried, they just waved at us to walk faster. I picked up the pace and followed him.

"Whatever they're going to show us," Rachel mumbled, "it better be good."

But it wasn't good at all.

We veered off the official marked path and snaked around a collapsed figure of a pharaoh – at least he looked like a pharaoh to me. And then we stopped.

Eric was the first to express what I was already thinking. "What?" he said. "This is it?" He looked around the area we were standing in. "So this is where Hannah disappeared?"

"Anna," Rachel corrected.

We had stopped in probably the most *uninteresting* section of the whole open-air museum. At least the statue of the Nubian lion was worth taking a picture of. "Soooo," I said, "you guys want us to start looking around for Anna?"

It seemed crazy to just walk about calling Anna's name. In fact, I doubted she was even here. Not once did either man call her name, or even look around for her on the long walk to this place. I started wondering if the scientists weren't a little crazy themselves.

Dr. Wassler put down his bag next to one of three stones that formed the shape of a triangle. Rachel wriggled out of her backpack and carefully placed it next to his. She was still worried about damaging her e-book reader.

We waited for one of them to tell us what was going on.

Dr. Wassler walked to the center of the triangle

formed by the pillars, looked up at the sun, and then returned to where we were standing. "Do these petroforms look familiar to the three of you?"

We looked at one another, and then at the four-foot-high rocks. Each pillar looked sort of like a thick stone tube with a flat hat on top, if you know what I mean. "Nope," I said.

"No," Rachel repeated.

"You gotta be kidding," Eric grumbled. "We told you we've never been here before, so why would those things look familiar to us?" He pointed at the rocks like they were responsible for this whole misadventure.

Rudi indicated the pillar closest to us and said, "Please look again. This is important."

Eric didn't bother looking at the stone monument, or whatever it was. "You guys have been in the sun *way* too long," he said.

Rachel pretended to examine the pillars more closely. After glancing at the German men's dejected faces, I kind of felt bad for them, so I looked at the pillars along with her. A minute later, Rachel raised her head and said, "They don't look familiar to me, Rudi." She turned to Rudi's brother. "Sorry, Dr. Wassler."

"Please, call me Bruno," he said.

I knew Rachel was probably expecting me to raise my head in agreement, but I couldn't – not yet anyway. Because something *did* appear familiar. "Give me a second to think," I said.

Eric rolled his eyes – he probably thought I was still

faking interest – and walked over to the fallen pharaoh carving, but Rachel was intrigued. "What is it, Cody?"

"I'm not sure," I said, stepping back and staring at the pillar. "But doesn't this look like one of the tombstones in the Sultana Cemetery?"

Rachel had an awesome memory and I knew I could count on her to remember. She walked around the chest-high stone twice and then stopped. "It does look kind of like that one next to *The Funny Guy*."

Because of our prank, we had to perform community service all around Sultana, including mowing the graveyard back home. After two weeks, we had stopped getting creeped out by the tombstones, and even started referring to some areas in terms of the interesting grave markers close by. We stored the extra gas cans near *The Alphabet Guy*, whose name had every letter. We took our breaks in *The French Quarter*, where all the French-sounding graves were clustered together under the big oak trees. And we usually had lunch by *The Funny Guy*, because his grave was elevated and made a nice picnic table. Sure, it was kind of morbid, but we didn't think the dead people minded. After all, we were keeping the place looking nice for them.

Anyway, we were told that we had to cut the grass one more time before we left for Egypt – that was two days ago. And I had taken some practice pictures with my new camera. "Wait a minute!" I said.

The scientists shifted impatiently while I removed my camera from my pocket. I turned it on and scrolled back to the first few pictures I had taken. "No way!" I said, staring at a picture of Eric, who was clutching his neck and pretending he was choking. Next to him was *The Funny Guy's* headstone, which said:

Chester Bassani

1899 – 1963

"I told you I was sick"

But that wasn't what grabbed my attention. In the photo next to Eric, beside *The Funny Guy's* headstone, stood a pillar that looked exactly like the ones here in Egypt.

"I can't believe it!" Rachel said, looking at the picture with me. "There really is a grave just like this in Sultana."

"It's not a headstone," Bruno said. "It's an ancient astronomical marker."

"What?" I raised my head.

"And," Bruno added, "We have seen all *three* markers in Sultana."

"There are three?" Rachel asked.

"Yes," Rudi said. "They are placed exactly as they are here – the same orientation, the same distance, the same shape."

"You failed to notice the other two markers because they are obscured by dense brush and trees." Bruno seemed pleased that we were paying attention now. "But all three are there. We've seen them."

"So they're *not* graves?" Rachel asked.

"No," Bruno said. "They have been there for

thousands of years – perhaps tens of thousands. Settlers to the area likely imagined they were gravestones, and over time it became a community cemetery. But they are not tombs."

"That's all pretty interesting," I said, and I meant it. "But what does that have to do with us, or your daughter's disappearance?"

Bruno nodded and said, "I will show you." He seemed to relax a little and added, "Thank you for listening. I know this will sound extraordinary at first." He waved us over to the nearest pillar and pointed at a symbol carved into the stone, near the base. "Do you see this glyph?" he asked.

We nodded at the odd image of several strange shapes surrounded by a box. Since I still had my camera in my hand, I snapped a few pictures of the chiseled object.

"This is a Mayan calendar symbol," Bruno said. "And it can't be found anywhere else in Egypt."

Rachel nodded.

"So why is that a big deal?" I asked.

"The 'big deal'," Rudi said, "is that the Mayans lived in Southern Mexico and Northern Central America. They were *never* in Egypt."

"Oh," I said.

Bruno brushed off another area of the stone with what looked like a paintbrush. "And do you see this chiseled text?" He tapped the worn characters. "These are Chinese symbols from the Han Dynasty – the second century BC. They never traveled here either."

Eric wandered back to join us. He had perked up after hearing about the gravestones in Sultana. "What about these?" he asked, pointing at some plaster etchings near the top. "Where are they from?"

"Ah, yes," Bruno said, "I was going to show you those next." He brushed sand from the cracks and then sprinkled water onto the stone from his bottle. "This style is typically seen at Native American sites."

Eric and Rachel each took a turn looking at the sequence of engravings, while I took another photo.

"These three stones," he continued, "have glyphs and text from a dozen different cultures – Incan, Mayan, Druid, Native American, Aztec, Khmer, Egyptian, and the list goes on and on. Yet nowhere in recorded history do we have evidence of these people ever being in Egypt – except the Egyptians, of course."

He had our attention now, and I was about to say something, when he really threw a curve ball at us.

"And those three stones in Sultana – in your home town – also have symbols from people and cultures that have never been to North America. Or so the world thinks."

"Whoa!" Eric said.

"Wait a minute," I said. "You mean the pillars in our cemetery look like that?" I pointed at the glyph-covered stone.

"Absolutely," Rudi said. "They are more faded, covered in moss, and obscured with lichen – you have a different climate in Canada – but each stone there also has ancient glyphs, symbols, and codes. Some messages are etched in a coating of mortar, some are chiseled or carved into the stone, and few are even painted."

"And some of the symbols," Bruno added, "are dates that make reference to time periods before or well after that culture existed. Some of the Mayan dates *overlap* the dates referenced by the Chinese Han Dynasty. This should be impossible because the Mayans existed one thousand years *before* that dynasty."

"But how can that be?" Rachel asked. "How can the stones in our graveyard back home be decorated by people from so many places, from such different time periods?"

Bruno looked up at the sun again and then down at his wristwatch.

"Yeah," Eric said. "And if both stone sites are real – like you say they are – wouldn't this be a huge deal? Wouldn't *all* archaeologists be talking about it? I never heard about Egyptians coming to Sultana, until *we* made it up." He grinned fiendishly at the memory.

"Many people know about the sites," Rudi said. "But no one wants to talk about it, because no one wants to consider the most logical explanation."

I looked up. "What's that?"

"Time travel," Bruno answered somberly.

Eric stared at him. "No wonder no one is listening to you two."

Eric had a point – the scientists sounded nuttier

and nuttier the more they explained – but I *had* seen these pillars in Sultana. "What do you mean about time travel? What does that have to do with anything?"

"What do you know about atoms?" Rudi asked.

I sighed – it sounded like Rudi was trying to change the subject. Rachel, feeling more indulgent, decided to go along with him. "They're super-small and they make up everything," she offered quickly.

Rudi nodded. "Good. And atoms are made up of many even smaller *subatomic*, or *quantum* particles."

"Okay," I said.

"Sure," said Rachel.

"Whatever," said Eric.

"And," Rudi continued, "in laboratory studies these quantum particles are always appearing and disappearing."

"So?" Eric said.

"So where do they go?" Rudi asked.

"I don't know," Eric said, getting frustrated. "This is your story."

"Many physicists believe that the particles can – and *do* – travel back and forth in time."

"Okay ... that's all very interesting," I said. "But we still don't know what any of *that* has to do with these pillars or Anna disappearing ..."

"And why are *we* here?" Eric asked.

Rudi and Bruno looked at each other, then again at the sky.

"We have a theory," Rudi said, "that every once in

a while – under the right conditions – the *past* bumps and touches and rubs against the *present*. And when the timeline of history is affected this way, something incredible happens."

"What's that?" Rachel said, sounding fascinated.

"We think a window – sometimes called a wormhole – opens up that permits people or objects to move back and forth along the timeline. We have moved quantum particles forward in time using laboratory equipment, and we believe the ancients time traveled using the pillars."

Eric shook his head. "And you guys thought my prank theory was nutty," he muttered.

"But how?" I asked. "What happened to Anna?"

Rudi emptied a whole bottle of water into his mouth and took one giant swallow. "We think that there is one timeline – one history – for everything that has ever happened here on Earth. And we believe the pillars identify precise wormholes that will take a person back to specific moments on that timeline."

Bruno must have thought we were confused, though I was still trying to figure out if these guys were for real. "Think of the stones as the first signposts placed along a time traveler's highway," he said. He paused and waited for us to respond. I didn't know what else to do, so I nodded like I understood what he meant.

"Perhaps some thousand years ago," he went on, "an Egyptian just vanished while chasing his sheep. Or a Chinese stone mason disappears while gathering rocks for the Great Wall. Over the millennia, the ancients begin to see patterns emerge and start documenting their 'travel' experiences – or warnings, I suppose – on the surface of the pillars."

Rudi grinned. "These pillars are like a giant time traveler's owner's manual, written in a dozen languages."

"And now you want to use the stones," Rachel kicked the same pillar Rudi had kicked, "to go back in time and get Anna?"

"Yes," Rudi said.

Bruno saw Eric shake his head. "There are other more experimental methods we could use. But this one is the easiest."

"What do you mean?" I said. "Are you saying there are *other* ways to time travel?"

"Most certainly," Rudi said, "There are Walker Cylinders, Teetaert Horizons, Leroux Tunnels, and even Schleckem Entanglements. Any of these technologies *could* be used to travel back in time, but we need to travel to a very specific point on an unimaginably long timeline. And we need to do it *now*."

"That doesn't make any sense," Eric said.

"Yes it does, Eric," Rudi said. "Why would we want to use relatively *unreliable* Schleckem Entanglements to get Anna, when we can use these pillars?"

Eric stared. "No, I didn't mean the Schleckem thing. I mean this is *all* crazy." He waved his arms around the whole area, making sure he included the brothers.

The scientists exchanged a glance, and Rachel glared at her brother. "So you have no idea *where* in the past Anna landed?" she asked.

"Because the timeline of history goes all the way back to the Big Bang, and even that is a theory, she could be anywhere. She might be with the Egyptians. She also might be in a jungle where there are no people. Or she may have traveled to some period in prehistory we can't even imagine."

"My guess is she's in Egypt," Eric said, trying to be helpful. "If a person really *did* disappear from here, it would make sense that they would reappear here too – but in the past, I suppose."

"That would be nice," Bruno said, "but it's not so simple. The Earth is constantly spinning right under our feet. The alignment of the planets and the sun will likely occur in a different location, wherever Anna is in the past, than it did here today. So she could be at *any* of the pillar sites."

We stood around in a circle with one of the pillars in the middle, and no one said anything for a long time. I didn't believe anything they were telling us, of course, but if it was true, Anna was in big trouble.

Rachel broke the silence. "I hate to say it, but if she could be anytime and anywhere in the past, how do *you* expect to find her?"

"Luckily all those ancient cultures marked the pillars with glyphs and symbols. And those are the clues." Bruno shook his head. "But unfortunately, Anna vanished yesterday before I could tell her their meaning. If she knew what I now know she could even come back on her own."

"But how did she disappear?" Rachel asked.

"Yeah," Eric said. It sounded to me like he didn't believe a word of this story either. "What was she doing when she disappeared?"

Rudi walked to the center of the triangle formed by the three pillars. "Anna was helping us measure the distance from pillar to pillar so that we could triangulate the exact center of the petroform site. The last time we saw her she was standing here." He looked down at his fourteen-inch shoes and frowned. "After she vanished –"

I cut him off. "What exactly do you mean by 'vanished'?"

"She was telling us that she found the geometric center of the petroform, when suddenly she disappeared. There was a sharp electrical snapping sound, and Anna was gone."

"Riiiiiight," Eric said, "she just fell down into some wormhole and never returned."

Bruno was on his knees, digging around in his rucksack for something. Rudi walked back to where we were standing.

"I think I've heard enough," I whispered to Eric, "These guys really are a bit loony. Let's get out of here *now*."

Eric nodded. "Yeah, they can even keep my luggage for all I care."

Rachel walked over to the center of the stones. Apparently, she hadn't given up on the scientists yet. "So she was standing here one minute," she said, "and the next minute ..."

"NOOOOO!" Bruno bellowed. He jumped up, turned around, and dropped his water bottle.

But it was too late.

There was an electrical snap and Rachel was gone. I couldn't believe it. When I saw it happen on TV and in the movies, I *knew* it wasn't real. But this time I witnessed it with my own eyes.

She had vanished.

CHAPTER 4

"What have you done?!" Eric screamed. "Where is my sister? Get her back now!"

Bruno looked shocked. He ignored Eric and started mumbling. "Oh no ... oh no, no, no. This is a nightmare – terrible."

I yanked on his arm and said, "What just happened? How do we bring her back? Tell us what to do!"

Rudi picked up his brother's fallen water bottle, opened it, and made Bruno take a drink. He guided him to a collapsed column of stone and encouraged him to sit down.

Bruno was shaking pretty badly but he recovered enough to talk. "I was about to ask if one of you would fetch Anna, but now this ..."

"Now what?!" Eric screamed.

"Rachel doesn't know the secret to return either. I was about to tell you, but it all happened so fast ..." Bruno gave Eric a mournful look. "She doesn't know about the solstice. Now they're both gone ... both trapped in the past."

"Is there a problem here?" I looked up to see two Egyptian park police officers coming toward us – they didn't look happy. "What is all the yelling about?"

Eric turned around and said, "Yeah, there's a

problem –"

I jabbed him in the kidney before he could finish. "Don't say anything," I whispered, "or we won't be able to get Rachel back."

"Huh?" Eric was red-faced and still furious, but at least I had his attention.

"If we tell the police Rachel just *vanished*, they'll lock us all up, or send us home, or something. Just be cool until we find her."

The cops came closer and gave each of us a good once-over. The older officer glared at Eric and said, "Is something wrong here?"

Eric looked at me and then back at the cop. "Yes, there is," he said. "I was playing kick tag with my uncles and they cheated." Eric gave Bruno and Rudi each a good kick in the shins and laughed. "You're *it* now."

Both scientists winced and then laughed too.

The uniformed man probably thought the heat had gotten to us. He shook his head wearily. "Please try and stay on the marked trails," he said. "This is not a playground, it's a museum. There is nothing of importance in this section." Both men turned around and walked away. I saw the older cop flip open a cell phone and speak rapidly in Arabic.

When the park patrol disappeared, Eric quickly asked, "Okay, so how can we get Rachel back?"

Bruno wiped his brow with his wrist. "The window has closed for today. We'll have to try again tomorrow – if the wormhole is still there."

"Tomorrow? Are you insane? We can't leave Rachel – wherever she is – alone until tomorrow. We have to find her now!"

"Yeah," I said. "Just tell us how to get Rachel – and Anna – back. We'll go right now."

Rudi pointed at me and said, "*You* cannot go at all, Cody. Only Eric can go."

"What? Just try and stop me!"

"No," Rudi said, "you misunderstand. You can't go because you're not thirteen yet – Eric and Rachel are."

"So?" Eric said.

Bruno rubbed his shin and then pointed at the nearest pillar. "There are two ideas that are repeated in the symbols and glyphs we have translated so far. The summer solstice and a very specific astronomical event."

"Do you know about the solstice?" Rudi asked.

We both shook our heads.

"On June twenty-first of each year the sun reaches its highest point in the sky. And it even *appears* to stand still for several minutes before continuing. This happens for three or four days in a row, and then the days get shorter again. Today – in fact, only five minutes ago – we had the summer solstice here in Egypt."

"Okay," Eric said, sounding determined. "What do we do now?"

"We will come back tomorrow," Bruno said. "And when the sun is at its highest point and casts no shadow, you can travel to the past, where Anna and Rachel are. Find them, bring them back to the markers where you

59

arrived, and wait for the summer solstice in that place. Then the three of you can come back – safe and sound."

"What if he misses the solstice?" I asked. "What if it's already happened where the girls are?" I didn't want to be a pessimist, but they were making it all sound way too simple.

Rudi and Bruno looked at each other. "It's possible," Rudi admitted. "But we have to start with the most logical theory – that if you hurry, you will arrive at a portal that is linked to this wormhole. And *that* wormhole will remain usable for as long as the one on this end."

"This is one hundred percent nuts," Eric said. Then he stared at the spot where Rachel had disappeared. It was the first time I had seen my normally laid-back friend look so serious. "But I guess I don't really have a choice," he finished quietly.

"Do you think we should call your mom?" I asked. "Or my parents – you know, let them know what's going on?"

"No way!" Eric shot back. "My mom will go totally bonkers."

"But she might be able to help – call the Canadian Embassy, or the police, or something."

Three hours had passed and we were now sitting on our beds in a tiny, minus-three-star motel room on the edge of Memphis. Rudi had left to find us some food, and Bruno was in the next room pacing around and grumbling to himself. He ignored us.

"She probably would make lots of phone calls," Eric admitted, "but nothing she could do will help Rachel or Anna. We have to sort this out on our own."

I agreed with him, and it was a relief to hear him say what I had already been thinking. There really was no way *anyone* would accept what we saw today. If we called the police or an embassy, we would all just be locked up and questioned for days and days. No one would ever believe Anna and Rachel had vanished into thin air – that's crazy talk.

And if we didn't get Eric to those pillars by high noon tomorrow, it would be too late for the girls – maybe forever.

How did we get into these situations?

"Hey, Bruno," Eric called. He wandered over to our room looking pretty exhausted. I guess he wasn't having a great day either.

He pulled up a chair and sat down. "I'm very sorry about all this, boys."

Eric acknowledged his apology with a few quick nods. "You never really answered our question in the car. Why did you try to steal our fake tablet back in Sultana?"

Bruno laughed for the first time that day. "Ironically, it was your tablet that started this whole affair."

"How do you figure that?" I asked.

"Yeah," Eric shot back, "why are you blaming us for this mess?"

"Well," Bruno said, "we've been watching *all* the sites for years –"

"Hold it!" Eric cut him off. "Where are these other pillars anyway?"

"Oh," he said in surprise, like it was obvious. "The same stone formations, with similar glyphs, have been located in Peru, Southern Mexico, Cambodia, China, and England. We always believed a site would be found in North America. So when the *Ebenezer Project* heard about the tablet in Sultana, we got very excited."

"Why's that?" Eric asked.

"Because if a *real* Egyptian plaque was actually found in Sultana it would have confirmed our theory of a time travel portal. Anyway, Rudi and I quickly flew to your home town to search the area for similar pillars, and we were not disappointed. The astronomical markers were right there in the cemetery. We were ecstatic."

"So, you *suspected* there might be pillars in North America," I said, "but it wasn't until you heard about an Egyptian tablet being found in Manitoba that you located them?"

"Correct," Bruno said. He gave us a sheepish grin. "We knew that the native North American symbols on the pillars resembled glyphs found in central Canada – Manitoba, to be precise. So we estimated, or guessed, that there might also be pillars somewhere in Manitoba. And when we heard about the plaque ..."

"But why were you trying to steal it?" I asked again.

"One of our earlier theories involved the use of dark matter or some other anti-energy to open the portal and allow time travel along the timeline. We thought that if we could take the plaque we could analyze and test it in Rudi's laboratory. But of course, that theory is crazy."

"Not like everything else," Eric mumbled.

"Pardon me?" Bruno said.

"Nothing."

"Okay," Eric said, "I'll eat this stuff because I'm hungry and it smells good. But I don't want anyone telling me what it is. I don't need to know if it's dead goat, or pickled lamb, or boiled pigeon, or whatever."

Rudi laughed and continued to open boxes, spreading them around on the table in the kitchen area. "Just eat," he said. He had returned to our motel room with a large bag of foodstuff.

Eric and I must have been starving, because we couldn't stop stuffing our faces. Rudi waited and didn't touch anything until the three of us had finished, and then he ate what was left. And believe me, there was a lot left. Man, could he eat! We watched in fascination as he pounded down enough calories to feed a village.

"I think we need more gear," I announced when the men had made coffee for themselves and returned to the table.

"Oh," Bruno said, puzzled. "What kind of gear?"

I looked down at the list Eric and I made in the bedroom. We were pretty worried that the brothers had made everything sound *too* simple. Maybe they were just acting optimistic so we wouldn't freak out, but we wanted backup equipment in place. Nothing was ever as straightforward as an adult made it sound.

"First of all," I said, "we want a world phone."

"A what?" Rudi asked, sipping his coffee.

"A satellite phone," Eric said, "one that will work from anywhere on Earth."

Big Rudi shook his big head. "That won't help you in the past."

"We know that," I said. "But what about when we return? What if we come back through the pillars in Cambodia, or on a mountaintop in Peru? Don't you think we should call you when we get back with Anna?"

"Mein Gott! My God!" Bruno said. "I never even considered that. Absolutely we will get you that phone." He found his own notepad and began patting his pockets, searching for a pen. Rudi pointed to the side of his head and his brother took the hint. Bruno pulled a pen from behind his ear and said, "What else have you thought of?"

"Eric will take two backpacks with him," I said. "Both will be loaded with food and clothes – one for Rachel and Anna, and one for Eric. The girls will be hungry, and they may be cold. We have Rachel's clothes, but you should give us stuff for Anna, unless she's the same size."

"Yes, yes, good," Bruno kept taking notes. "And what else?"

I looked at my list again. "A first aid kit, a flashlight, a small folding pocketknife, duct tape, matches, and maybe a lighter."

"Excellent ..." He kept writing.

"And a pair of walkie-talkies," I said, "with extra batteries."

Rudi and Bruno exchanged confused expressions.

I sighed, "A handheld, portable, two-way radio."

"Ahhh," Bruno said. "*Sehr gut*. Very good."

Eric coughed and cleared his throat. "And for protection ... I need a gun."

Rudi choked on his coffee. "What?!"

"Absolutely not!" Bruno said.

I'd told Eric earlier that they wouldn't go for the gun, but he was determined. "I don't plan on hurting anyone. I just need something to keep us safe until we get out of there. From wild animals and stuff." I thought that was pretty reasonable, but the scientists didn't look convinced. "Look, I'm going to travel back in time tomorrow, to a world that's probably dangerous. I don't know any Karate or Kung Fu or anything like that, and I want *something* in case of ... in case of an emergency." Eric crossed his arms on his chest, to show he could be just as stubborn as the scientists.

It was a good argument, and they seemed to seriously consider the benefits of arming Eric. Their

German debate went on for a long time, and it looked like Bruno was winning the argument – although I don't know if he was *for* or *against* a weapon. Finally, they both nodded and turned to face us again.

"Rudi will give you the zapper," Bruno said.

Eric loved gadgets, but after how long the Germans had hesitated, he was a little suspicious. "The 'zapper'?"

Rudi gave his brother another look, and Bruno nodded in reply. He left the kitchen area and returned with the same handheld device – the thing they had used to trick Aubey – we were shown earlier in the car. "This," he said, "delivers just enough electricity to stun a person for two to five minutes. But you have to be close enough to touch the person – or animal, I suppose. The trigger is the power switch, there are no other settings."

"You mean there's no safety lock?" Eric asked.

Rudi nodded. "The safety switch is part of the handle, and the power will not turn on unless you hold the zapper like this." Rudi showed Eric how to hold the device. "By grabbing the zapper properly the built-in safety is bypassed and the trigger is ready. Simply touch the probe to a person and then push the plunger."

Eric reached out, eager to hold it, but Rudi packed it away again. Maybe he thought we would zap them both and leave. I have to admit, the idea crossed my mind.

"Its limitation is that it can only be used four times," Bruno cautioned while Rudi hid the zapper. "Do not waste those four charges."

I gave Bruno the rest of our list, which he transferred to his book. He then added some other items and gave the shopping list to Rudi. Rudi finished his coffee and left again.

When the door closed, Bruno turned to us with an apologetic look on his face. He opened and closed his mouth several times before he started speaking. "The *Ebenezer Project*," he began slowly, "has been researching and monitoring these sites for over a decade and –"

I held up my hand and Bruno stopped. "Wait – why did you call it 'Ebenezer'?"

"Oh, I'm sorry," he said. "I should have explained that earlier. *A Christmas Carol* was my favorite story as a kid, and Ebenezer Scrooge was the first fictional character to time travel – a ghost took him to the future and the past. We thought it was a fitting title for our research on the stones."

Eric shook his head. He opened his mouth to comment, but decided not to.

"As I was saying, the *Ebenezer Project* was very close to solving the puzzle of the pillars when Anna vanished. Then everything changed. Getting Anna back became my priority. It was a coincidence that Aubey brought you to Egypt just when she disappeared, but I needed your help urgently. I'm sorry if we scared you."

I pinched the bridge of my nose, like I'd seen Rudi do several times. "Well, why didn't you just *ask* for our help?"

"Ahh, yes, Cody, a very good question. I called Aubey this morning, asking him to help us get Anna back, but he didn't believe what we told him."

Eric and I looked at each other. I guess that explained Aubey's overcautious behavior at the airport.

Bruno continued. "Aubey *was* interested in learning about the pillars, but he said my plan put the three of you in too much danger. It also didn't help that he works for our opposition. So we had to ... *borrow* you – but only to get Anna back."

"That's just great," I said.

"Yeah," Eric grumbled. "Thanks for getting us involved in your bizarre science project."

Bruno seemed to not hear us and went on. "When I told Aubey that Anna vanished on her thirteenth birthday –"

"– Wait a sec!" Eric sat up straight. "It's *my* birthday today and it's Cody's the day after tomorrow." I think Eric didn't remember he had turned thirteen today until now. That's what happens when you get your presents ahead of time, I guess. A birthday isn't a birthday if you don't get cake and presents on *that* day.

"Of course it is," Bruno said. "I saw your passports and I know that. You will all be thirteen in two days. That's why I needed your help."

"But why *us*?" I asked. "Why'd you have to pick us and ruin *our* holiday?"

Bruno sighed. "I had no choice – we didn't have much time to find anyone else. We knew you would be in Egypt *and* you happened to be the same age as my daughter. Also, you have shown yourselves to be courageous and resourceful – remember, I saw your plaque too – and very smart."

"I suppose that makes sense," I said, even though I wasn't sure it made *any* sense.

Eric looked like he was in a trance. Bruno had been talking for so long, I think Eric was now completely confused. "But if my birthday is today, can I still get her and Rachel back tomorrow?"

"Absolutely," he said. "Don't lose heart. Here on Earth your birthdays may be celebrated on a very specific day – each only twenty four hours long. But astronomically, you were all born during the same amazing cosmic event. And that event lasted for three or four days."

I tried hard to process what I just heard. "So if *my* birthday is the day after tomorrow," I said, "maybe I *can* still help Eric get Rachel and Anna. The window will allow me through too."

Bruno shrugged. "Maybe. But even if it does, I don't believe we should risk sending you both."

"But it's *my* risk," I said. "And I want to go help Eric get the girls. We can do a better job as a team."

Eric nodded.

"Please listen," Bruno said. "If you had both jumped into the wormhole right after Rachel, you would all four be together. Correct?"

"Yeah ..." Eric said.

"And we'd be much better off than we are now," I added.

"No!" Bruno said. "You would all four be stuck in the past, and *none* of you would know how to come back. If you stay here with us, and Eric goes alone, then we still have someone to send through the wormhole if there are ... complications."

"There better not be complications," Eric grumbled.

"I know," Bruno agreed, "but if there are, we might be able to help on this end. We could unravel some of the other symbols and Cody might still be able to travel to you, and the girls, using a different event – one we don't know of yet."

I still wanted to go with Eric, but I kept my mouth shut. It *was* smarter for me to stay here, in case something happened. I looked over and saw Eric's anxious, worried face. I knew he'd prefer it if I went with him – but I also knew Bruno was right – he had to go alone.

The three of us remained silent for several minutes, until Eric asked, "What's this cosmic event, the thing you said is happening right now?"

"Every thirteen years, during the summer solstice, all the important planets – astrologically speaking, I mean – line up directly behind the sun. We can't see them, but when the sun is at its highest point in the sky, Mercury, Venus, Jupiter, and Saturn align to form a powerful singularity. Rudi and I believe *that* planetary event, combined with the summer solstice, causes the timeline of history to bend so much that the past bumps against the present."

He paused and took a long slurp of coffee.

"And that bump, of course," he continued, "opens the wormhole portal marked by the pillars."

I looked at Bruno and then at Eric. "And because the three of us were born during this special event thirteen years ago," I summarized, "we can use the stones to travel backward in time."

"Correct," said Bruno.

Goose bumps suddenly appeared on my arms. "Are you saying that if something does go wrong, Eric and the girls will be stuck in the past for thirteen years? And I'll have to wait until I'm twenty-six before I can even *attempt* to help them again?"

"Of course," Bruno said. "You can *only* use the wormhole during the cosmic anomaly."

Eric's already pale skin seemed to turn even whiter. "I got a bad feeling about all this," he said. "A real bad feeling."

CHAPTER 5

The next morning – after probably the worst sleep in my life – we both got up around nine. Eric looked like he may have slept even less than I had. His eyes were red and had developed heavy bags underneath, and sweat had plastered his blond hair against his head.

"What a night," I groaned.

"I think I might barf!" he said from the edge of his bed.

"Take a shower, you'll feel better," I said, and immediately cringed. I sounded like my mother. "I'll go see what kind of breakfast food they have for us."

After we both showered and ate, we decided we'd better check in and phone home. Eric called his mom first and put on a great show of pretending everything was awesome – "Just fantastic," he kept repeating. At one point, when Mrs. Summers asked to speak with Rachel, Eric said, "Ahh, no ... she's not here right now ... she's swimming in the hotel pool." He rambled on a bit about the full schedule Aubey had planned, and how we might not be able to call them every day.

It was easier for me because I connected with our answering machine. I left what I hoped was a friendly-sounding message, similar to what Eric had said. My mind was swamped with worry and panic, so I was glad I didn't have to have an extended conversation with Mom and Dad. Especially if I had to lie all the way through it.

Anyway, we didn't have a lot of time to waste. The four of us sorted through all the equipment Eric was going to take. We crammed everything into the backpacks except for the satellite phone, which wasn't ready yet. Rudi said it was being programmed and he would have to go back to the store to pick it up.

"I'll drop you three off at Mit Rahina," he said, "and then I will get the phone."

I frowned. "Well, are you going to make it back to the pillars before the solstice?"

"I'll try my best," Rudi said. "I know the phone is important – I'll hurry."

"But if the electronics store doesn't have the phone ready," Bruno said, "you'll have to go without it."

Eric groaned. "This isn't a good start."

An hour later we were back in the parking lot of the open-air museum at Mit Rahina. A nervous-looking Rudi dropped us off with the backpacks and a cooler of water bottles and snacks. "Don't worry," he assured us, "I'll return as soon as possible."

We watched as Rudi tore up the gravel and sped north toward Cairo. It was still too early for the tour buses, visitors, and vendors, so we had the ruins to ourselves. When the dust began to settle, Eric and I each shouldered a backpack and made our way down the trail to the pillars.

When we got to the stones, we slumped down in the shade of a thick limestone column. But its shadow was rapidly vanishing as the sun climbed to its highest point in the sky – the solstice.

Bruno wandered among the pillars, glancing at his wristwatch every few minutes. I know he was thinking what we were thinking: *Where the heck was Rudi?*

We had our backs against the cool stone and stared in horror as our patch of shade on the dirt quickly disappeared. "How much longer do you think we have?" Eric asked.

I shook my head. "Maybe twenty minutes."

Eric moaned, pulled his legs closer to his body, and began rocking back and forth.

I waved Bruno over and he settled down on the ground in front of us. His eyebrows lifted a bit and he said, "Yes?"

I wanted to distract Eric from his worries, so I asked Bruno something that had been on my mind all morning. "Yesterday you told us that Aubey was working for someone else – for the opposition. What did you mean by that?" I asked.

That grabbed Eric's attention and he stopped staring at the shadows around us. "Yeah," he said, "is he your enemy or something? He seems okay."

According to the scientists, Aubey had tried pretty hard to protect us from them, so he must be a decent guy. Sure, he was a bit strange, but he was also responsible for giving us twenty-five thousand dollars and arranging our trip to Egypt. It wasn't his fault that Anna had disappeared.

Bruno frowned at the time displayed on his watch. "Aubey is a conscientious Egyptologist, but the organization he works for is not as ethical as it once was."

"What do you mean?" Eric asked.

"He is employed by EAL – Egyptian Antiquities Limited. They used to do honorable work preserving Egypt's amazing culture and heritage. But then they learned about these pillars." Bruno pointed at the stones over his shoulder.

"I thought everyone knew about them?" I asked.

"True, but only Rudi, me, and EAL believe the stones may be markers for a doorway to the past. When they realized the potential of traveling to the past, they became very greedy."

"Greedy for what?" Eric asked.

Bruno placed a pebble on the edge of the shadow cast by the column behind us. "Imagine how much money could be made if you could travel back to ancient Egypt. Imagine if you could bring back treasures from that world and sell them now – today. Collectors will pay exorbitant amounts for such artifacts and art. EAL knows that and they want to exploit those ancient cultures."

"But if they traded with or paid the people from the past for the stuff," I asked, "is it such a big deal?"

"Maybe," Bruno said. "But that's not their plan. And, anyway, *any* interaction with the past – or with *any* ancient civilization – could have devastating consequences."

"For them, you mean?" I asked.

"No, for everyone – for the past, for the present, *and* for the future. You should just find the girls and come back. Don't linger."

Eric opened his mouth to say something, but I think his throat was too dry and no sound came out. He licked his lips, swallowed hard, and tried again. "Okay," was all he said.

"It's time to get ready, Eric." Bruno announced. He looked at his watch one last time and then up at the sun, high above us now.

"But what about the satellite phone?" Eric said, "I can't leave without that."

"I know it's important," Bruno said, "but we can't wait any longer." He grabbed one of the backpacks and started walking to the center of the pillars. "Today is the third day of the full planetary alignment. And tomorrow will likely be the last. You have to find Anna and Rachel – and you have to get them back here within twenty-four hours."

I picked up the other bag and followed Bruno. I looked behind me and saw Eric follow reluctantly. He wanted Rachel back but he sure wasn't looking forward to disappearing to who-knows-where.

"Stand here," Bruno told Eric, pointing to a spot

on the ground. "It will begin in the next three or four minutes."

I noticed that Eric's hands were shaking, so I helped him put his backpack on and then clicked the straps in place. We placed the second pack down by his feet so he could quickly grab it. "Don't worry," I joked, "you'll probably be back in an hour." It wasn't enough, but the only thing I could do for my friend was help him relax.

Eric smiled weakly. "Can we go to McDonalds then and get a nice hamburger?"

Bruno and I stood back a few paces and waited for Eric to vanish. "It should happen any minute now," he said.

Just then, we heard a shout and pounding feet. We turned and saw that it was Rudi, running down the trail and into the clearing. Eric's face relaxed as soon as he saw him.

Then another figure appeared behind Rudi – a silhouette I recognized immediately. It was Aubey, and he was hot on Rudi's heels!

"I have the phone!" Rudi yelled. "I have it!" He sprinted across the clearing with a dented box under his arm.

Aubey caught up to Rudi as he neared us and dove at his legs. Rudi's massive body thumped to the ground, kicking up a plume of sand and dust. The two rolled over and over in a violent struggle. The satellite phone flew from Rudi's hands and he groped frantically to recover it again, while Aubey struggled to get on top of him.

I'm sure Aubey thought he was doing the right thing – trying to rescue us. But his timing couldn't have been worse. Eric needed the phone *now* – before he vanished like Rachel.

"STOP IT!" I yelled. "AUBEY! IT'S OKAY!"

Neither man seemed to hear, and the dusty brawl continued.

I raced forward and pounced on Aubey's back. "STOP!" I shouted as loudly as I could into his ear.

That worked. As soon as he released his vice-like grip on Rudi's legs, I jumped off. He crawled toward Eric, panting and coughing on dust.

Rudi found the satellite phone and fumbled with the packaging.

Aubey looked like a gravelly mess. "Thank goodness ... you are safe," he mumbled. He slowly stood up and patted us both on our shoulders awkwardly, and then looked around. "Where ... where is Rachel?"

"She disappeared," I said, staring at his bloody nose. "Just like Anna."

"So, it's all true, what Dr. Wassler told me yesterday morning? And what Rudi tried to tell me in the parking lot?" Aubey looked stunned, and then suddenly guilty. "I'm sorry. I didn't know. I fought with Rudi to find you ... back there ... He said you were safe but I thought maybe ... and I tried to track you down sooner but ..."

"It's all right, man," Eric said in a rush. "Fill us in later. Right now I have to get my sister."

I was starting to get a picture, though, of what had happened. Aubey must have seen Rudi back in the parking lot, and then confronted him about our abduction. And that was when their duel began.

Aubey recovered his breath and his senses. He turned and faced Eric. "Be very careful," he said. "I never believed the rumors until now ... but if everything you say is true ... I heard my company once sent someone through the stones –"

"– I think it may be starting!" I yelled, cutting him off. I could smell electricity or a static discharge – we all turned to face the pillars.

"HURRY!" Eric screamed. "I feel something happening too! Get me that stupid phone!"

Rudi ripped the satellite phone from the plastic cradle, took a step past his brother, and threw the phone toward us. I caught it, spun around, and jammed it into the second backpack, which Eric was now hugging.

And that was when we *both* fell into the wormhole.

I heard a loud bang of static electricity, followed immediately by a sensation of falling. At first it felt like I was sucked into some kind of waterspout, or tornado, or giant vacuum. After that, I just fell, but I didn't fall like I was being pulled by something – I fell slowly and endlessly. The whole thing could have lasted a few seconds, or it may have taken a month. Time had lost all bearing.

Then I felt a subtle change – a new sensation, like something was whizzing past as I fell. Could these be points in time on the unimaginably long timeline of history?

I began to panic.

What if we ended up in different places? What if I fell onto an island full of cannibals? What if Eric landed in Australia? What if we never saw each other, or Rachel, ever again? And *that* was when I really started to freak out.

So I did the only thing I could think of to make myself feel better – I screamed my face off.

"AHHHHH!"

CHAPTER 6

"Wake up," a voice begged. "Please, they will come back soon." The voice belonged to a girl – a girl who spoke with a German accent.

I ignored her and tried to return to the peace and quiet of my unconsciousness.

"Hurry!" the same voice said, getting more urgent. "We must leave this place now." I felt someone pulling my arm and then –

SLAP!

Ouch – that stung. I opened my eyes and saw a girl with short brown hair and big brown eyes kneeling in front of me. "Anna?" I asked, rubbing my cheek.

Her shoulders slumped. "Yes," she said, sounding relieved. "Did Papa send you?"

"Yeah," I felt too dizzy to stand, but I sat up and looked around the clearing for Eric. Only he wasn't there. "Oh no!" I groaned. *Where the heck did he end up?*

"Don't worry," Anna said, "your friend is over there, throwing up. He's very nauseated." Anna pointed to a cluster of pine trees on the edge of the clearing. I noticed her arm was scratched up and covered with bug bites.

"Don't you mean nauseous?" I said, and then quickly added, "That's good though – I mean, not that

81

he's throwing up, but that he's here."

Anna frowned. "No. I mean nauseated. Nauseous means 'something that causes nausea.'" She must have realized she was still pulling on my arm and let go of it. "We have to leave this place before they return."

Eric wobbled over on shaky legs. Lucky for him, he had missed the English lesson. "I feel awful," he moaned. "But am I ever happy you're here with me."

I tried to stand up too. "Yeah, and Bruno and Rudi were right about everything so far. We landed in the same place on the timeline as Anna. And the wormhole window *did* extend enough for me to pass through with you, even though my birthday isn't until tomorrow. Now I guess we just have to wait for tomorrow's solstice and leave with Anna and Rachel."

"I think they took her away," Anna said.

"What?" Eric asked.

"The girl. Rachel. Is she about my age with a blond ponytail?" Anna asked.

Eric and I stared at each other. "Yeah, that's exactly her," I said. "Have you seen her?"

"Yes," Anna said. She hesitated for a moment, looking almost guilty, like it was her fault Rachel wasn't with us now. "But as I said, they took her away," she repeated.

"Who took her?" Eric demanded.

"I don't know *who* they are." Anna looked nervously toward the west. "But we have to hide. Please. They'll come for you both soon. Your arrival made a lot of noise."

She was making me feel very edgy now. I scanned the forest around us for signs of danger. There didn't seem to be anything alarming, but Anna's fear was contagious.

"Okay," I said, picking up a backpack. "Show us where to go."

Eric snatched up the other bag and we followed Anna on our still-rubbery legs toward the east. Normally, it would have been an easy hike through open forest, but my chest felt unbearably tight. I suppose traveling through time can be hard on the body.

Anna stopped every few hundred feet so that Eric and I could catch our breath. I took the time to look around. Something niggled at the back of my mind – this place seemed so familiar, like I had been here before. I shook my head. Time traveling was hard on the senses too, I guess.

After about fifteen minutes we came to a river and took a longer break. I opened one of the backpacks and distributed some Egyptian energy bars. We watched as Anna eagerly devoured hers. Since Eric and I weren't really hungry – plus they actually looked kind of disgusting – we passed her ours too. She ate them almost as quickly as the first one.

"Thank you," she said.

I gave her a water bottle and waited for her to wash down the heavy bars. Eric walked over to the river bank and splashed his face.

I turned to Anna and introduced myself – in all the rush, we never had a chance to. "I'm Cody Lint, and that's my best friend, Eric Summers. The girl you saw – Rachel – is Eric's sister."

"I'm so sorry. I tried to save your sister ... but –"

Eric returned from the river. "It's okay. Just tell us what the heck's going on around here," he said.

Anna explained in detail what had happened to her since she vanished from the pillars at Mit Rahina. Fighting to control her emotions, she ended her story by describing how she had tried to wake Rachel but couldn't before they took her.

"You did the right thing," I said. "There's no point in you both being captured."

"Yeah," Eric agreed. "If you weren't there at the pillars today, we'd have no idea what happened to you or Rachel. We wouldn't even know if we were in the same time as Rachel."

"What did these guys look like – the people that grabbed Rachel?" I really wanted to know if we were dealing with cavemen, or Mongols, or –

"Did they look like cannibals?" Eric asked. I guess we were both thinking the same thing.

Anna raised her eyebrows at Eric. "No, no," she said. "They were nothing like that. They appeared to be native North Americans. In German we still say 'Indians.'"

"Are you sure?" I asked, though I was relieved to know we wouldn't be clubbed by cavemen.

"The ancient native tribes of North America are not really my specialty, but –"

Eric cut her off in mid-sentence. "Your *specialty*?" He rolled his eyes. "I thought you were thirteen."

"I am," Anna said, blushing. "Both my parents are archaeologists – and Uncle Rudi too. Every summer I travel with them and help them conduct their research on dig sites. Most of that experience has been researching ancient people in Egypt and the Middle East, but my parents have many books on native North Americans."

"And that's what the people who took Rachel looked like?" I asked.

"Yes," Anna nodded, "they look just like the pictures I have seen in my parents' textbooks."

Eric smacked a horsefly trying to bite the wet skin on the back of his neck. "What were they wearing?" he asked.

"They had straight black hair," she said. "All their clothing looked like it was made of animal hides and furs. I did not see any type of cloth. And they wore moccasins on their feet."

"Did they have huge headdresses on their heads?" Eric asked, rubbing the welt from the horsefly bite. "And were their faces painted with war paint?"

Anna looked back and forth between Eric and me. Maybe she thought Eric was teasing her. "I think that only happens in Hollywood movies. They seemed peaceful."

"Good," Eric said, "because we got enough problems."

Anna tried to swat some blackflies that were biting her already chewed-up ankles, but they were too fast.

I rummaged through my pack for insect repellent and passed it to Anna. "Thanks," she said. She squirted a big white blob on her hand and rubbed it all over her legs, arms, and face.

Meanwhile, I found Eric's GPS and turned it on to confirm what I suspected. The screen came alive and went through its start-up sequence, but after two minutes an error message said, *NO SATELLITES FOUND*. And how could it – there wouldn't be satellites up there for who-knew-how-long.

"That's too bad," I said, returning the GPS to an inside pocket. "It would have been nice to get a fix on our position."

"That's for sure," Eric said. "But at least we know we're in North America – in a boreal forest. And we have a river here, just like in –"

"– That's it!" I cried.

"Huh?" Eric said.

I had been looking up and down the river, wondering why the walk from the pillars seemed familiar. And then it hit me. "Guys – I know *exactly* where we are."

"What is it?" Anna said.

"This has to be Sultana – from five or six or seven hundred years ago, but still the place where our *future*

Sultana will be."

Eric didn't look convinced. "Just because there's a river down there doesn't mean this is Sultana."

"No," I said, "look around, Eric. Think about it. In our time, it takes about ten minutes to walk from the graveyard to the river. Right?"

Eric nodded. "Yeah..."

"Well, that distance is exactly the same as what we walked from the pillars here, to the river. That can't be a coincidence. I think we're looking at *our* MacFie River."

"I don't know ..." Eric said, sounding doubtful. "Wouldn't all the glaciers during the ice age have changed everything?"

"Well, yeah," I said, "but that's *way* before now. Remember what Mrs. Leavesley told us in school – geologically speaking, five hundred years or even a thousand years is like the blink of an eye. It's no time at all in the Canadian boreal forest."

Eric waved his arms through the air. "But what about the trees? They don't look the same."

"Sure, the trees look different – there will probably be a hundred forest fires here in the future – but the rock outcrops, and the shape of the river, and the features of the land are the same."

Eric stood up and reexamined our surroundings. I watched as he took in everything, and then slowly began nodding. "Holy smokes! I think you're right. I think that granite outcrop way back there is where they'll put the west end of the bridge hundreds of years from now."

"I can't be hundred percent sure," I said, looking at Anna. "But if that's the MacFie River, the Red River will be just around the corner. And if we walk west for a day or two, we should find the start of the prairie – the Great Plains. We're probably here long before any Europeans, but I think this is the forest around Sultana, Manitoba."

Anna nodded. "Okay ... I don't know this ... Sultana – it's your home?"

I was relieved she didn't think we had bashed our heads too hard somewhere in the wormhole. "Yeah – we were visiting Egypt from Sultana, before we got here."

Anna looked like she was about to ask something else, but Eric beat her to it. "This could help us find Rachel," Eric said. "All the houses and streets are missing, but we know this area like the back of our hands."

"Well, we used to, anyway," I said. "I'm sure all our favorite trails and shortcuts are gone, but yeah, the area is the same."

"At least Anna's dad was right about the time travel stuff. That means we shouldn't have trouble getting back," Eric said.

Anna's eyes widened. "What did Papa tell you?"

I remembered that Anna had no idea what had happened to her, so I filled her in. "Rudi and your dad figured out that the pillars are astrological markers that ancient people used to travel back and forth in time –

along the timeline."

Anna was quick. Right away, she asked, "Then why didn't Papa or Uncle Rudi come and get me?"

"It seems," Eric said, "only people who were born during a certain gastronomical event –"

Anna blinked. "– Do you mean *astronomical*?"

"Huh? Yeah, whatever," Eric continued. "Anyway, people who were born during a specific solstice event can use the pillars whenever it happens. But it only happens every thirteen years."

"That means you are both thirteen?" Anna asked.

"Eric and Rachel's birthday was yesterday," I said, "but mine is tomorrow."

"Well, at least you'll still have a chance to celebrate it," Anna said, smiling gently.

If we get back in time. "Yeah, though we had a small celebration before we left Sultana."

Anna grew quiet and seemed to be considering something. "Our birthdays are spread out over four days, so the cosmic alignment must last for several days."

Eric shrugged. "As long as it lasts for one more day – *today*."

"Your dad wanted Rachel to come here to bring you back," I said, "but we didn't really believe him until we saw Rachel disappear."

"At Mit Rahina?"

"Yeah," Eric said. "And now we're here to take you both back."

I looked at the shadows beneath the trees. "I think the solstice has already happened today, which means we have until tomorrow noon to find Rachel and get back to the pillars where we arrived."

"They will be searching for us too," Anna said, nervously looking at the dark forest behind us. She explained that when someone comes through the wormhole it makes an unbelievably loud noise. "They know that I'm here somewhere, and now they know you are here. For two days I have been hiding and trying to avoid the scouting parties that move through the area."

"How did you do it?" Eric asked, looking at the forest behind us. Like me, he was probably wondering how she could've survived on her own without any trouble. "Weren't you terrified?"

"Many of the archaeological sites I go to with my parents are in remote locations. We often stay in tents, and spend weeks at a time outside – like camping. I was frightened because of *how* I got here, but I am not frightened by a forest."

"Where did you hide?" I asked.

"And what did you eat?" Eric said. I rolled my eyes at him – of course he would ask that – and he shrugged.

"During the day – when I felt it was safe – I ate only wild strawberries. They are small but there are many of them. And at night I made a bed of branches from the cedar tree and covered myself with even more branches. The search party hasn't found me – but I think they know I'm here."

"I wonder what they want from you," I asked. "Or with us, or Rachel, for that matter."

"I don't think they mean any harm," Anna said. "Maybe they only want to protect us from danger – from the wild animals. But we can't be sure. I just want to go home."

You've got that right, I thought.

"Have you seen any wildlife?" Eric asked.

Anna nodded. "Oh, yes. I have seen many deer already – they are everywhere. And early this morning, when I climbed a tree to see the area better, I saw a family of foxes."

"But nothing like bears?" Eric asked, trying hard to sound casual. "Or wolves?"

She shook her head.

"So if they heard us land here," I said, getting back to our task, "then their village, or camp, or whatever, can't be too far away. That may work to our advantage, as long as we don't get caught first."

"Yeah," Eric said, smearing insect repellent on his own legs, "but we're from the twenty-first century and we've watched thousands of hours of TV. We can outsmart them."

I wasn't entirely sure about Eric's logic, but he did have a point. The local population was familiar with the area, but so were we. They would be trying to catch us, but we were on to them. Sure, they were adults and professional hunters, and we were just kids – but we were kids from the future.

"I think they will be behind us soon," Anna said. "We should move away from here." Since she had spent two days successfully avoiding capture, we trusted her gut instincts, and lifted our packs.

"Let's do what they do in the movies," Eric suggested. "We'll stomp down into the river, like we're crossing it and continuing north. But as soon as we're in the water, we'll turn and head south. They can't track us in water."

Anna nodded.

"That may not fool them forever," I said, "but it should buy us enough time to figure something out."

Twenty minutes later we were still on the same side of the MacFie River but about half a mile south. We slogged our way into the pine trees above the bank and rested. We all drank from our water bottles and ate from our supply of energy bars. Anna lost the look of fear and nervousness that showed on her face back at the stones. She told us about her father's and uncle's obsession with the pillars, and how every time they had the chance, they flew to one of the sites to examine and reexamine the curious markers.

"And that's why you were in Egypt?" I asked. "At Mit Rahina?"

"Yes." Anna took a sip from her water bottle and then nodded. "They often take me with them."

Eric found a comfortable looking place on the ground and sat down. "That is so cool," he said. "Flying all over the place and having all sorts of adventures."

I craned my neck and snuck a peek down the river to make sure we weren't being tailed. "Yeah," I agreed, "Egypt is the first place outside of Manitoba that we've ever been to ... and that was for less than a day. I mean, sure we traveled here to the past, but that doesn't even really count, because now we're back in Sultana."

Anna smiled, as if sympathizing.

"What about school?" Eric asked. "Don't you have to go to school in Germany or England or wherever you live?"

"Not anymore. I used to attend a school in Germany, but when Mama and Papa both got jobs at a university in England, they said I could be homeschooled."

"Are you kidding me?" Eric said. "You mean you never have to go to any boring classes?"

"I don't go to classes," Anna said, "but I still do all my lessons and assignments and tests."

"Come on," Eric teased, "really?" He popped a piece of the Egyptian bar into his mouth and grimaced each time he chewed.

"Yes, really. The only difference is that my home is my classroom, and I can do my studies from wherever my parents are – Egypt, Mexico, France ... anywhere."

"That's still pretty cool," I said, though I didn't think I'd be able to concentrate on my boring geometry homework when everything around me was so much more exciting.

Eric peeked around some willow shrubs to get a better view of the river downstream. Suddenly he froze. "There! There they are!" He pointed to where we had pretended to cross the river.

I dug out the binoculars Rudi had bought for us and crawled over to Eric. I zoomed in on the search party. "Five guys," I said, "no, make that six. And, Anna, I think you were right. Native North Americans." Anna joined us and I passed her the field glasses.

Anna sighed, looking at her pursuers. "Yes, that's them. They are the ones who took Rachel."

"Where could they have taken her?" I said to Eric. "If you had to set up a camp in Sultana – in *our* Sultana – where would you put it?"

Eric began snaking his way back to our packs. "Maybe by Bruce and Marg's house ..." He stopped and shook his head. "– I mean, where the MacFie River dumps into the Red River. The fishing there is good, and the bugs aren't too bad because of the constant breeze."

"Yeah," I agreed. "There really isn't a better place than that. And it would be close enough for them to hear whatever they heard when we arrived." I took a final glance downriver and watched with satisfaction as the search party moved north, checking for our tracks.

"Where is this place?" Anna asked.

Eric strapped on his backpack and pointed northwest.

Anna and I looked at the blue sky through a break in the forest above us. When I squinted, I saw fingers of light gray smoke drifting into the air, a mile from where we were standing.

Eric grinned. "That's a sure sign of a camp. We need to get there and take a look around."

I nodded. "But I don't think we should all go."

"You mean we should split up?" Anna looked stricken.

"Yeah," I said. "If the three of us go anywhere together as a group, our movements will scream out our presence to these guys. Remember, they're expert trackers and hunters. They'll see us, they'll hear us, and heck, they'll probably even smell us before we get within a hundred feet of their camp."

We sat quietly in the afternoon sun, contemplating our next move.

"I think I should go alone and check out their camp," I said. "See if Rachel's there."

Eric opened his mouth to protest but I cut him off. "My skin is way darker than yours. You almost glow in the night."

Anna looked at Eric's blond hair and pale skin, and then laughed. "It's true," she said. "And it's almost a full moon too. They might think you're a spirit and kill you if they see you tonight."

Eric didn't like the idea of being left out. "If I come," he said, "I could create a massive diversion while you rescue Rachel and –"

"– We're *not* rescuing her, not until we know what's going on," I reminded him. "And if two of us go, it only doubles the risk of us getting caught."

"He's right," Anna said. "Two people will make twice as much noise in the night. And the night here is very quiet – no wind, no birds, no other sounds. I could go, but you know this area, *and* it's dark. I might get lost."

So that settled it – I would wait until the sun had set, and I would have to be more careful than I'd ever been in my life.

CHAPTER 7

"More mud, Anna," Eric said. "And more moss and junk."

Anna and Eric were prepping me for my mission. I was standing in front of them wearing a dark brown T-shirt and khaki-colored shorts. Ten minutes ago my clothes looked brand-new – now they looked like I'd found them in a dumpster. Before I even put them on, we'd pounded both pieces of clothing with dirt and leaves, to get rid of any "foreign" smells.

We were now working on the finishing touches that would make my dark skin even darker. Anna smeared my legs with dirt, while Eric dripped sticky pine tree sap on my shirt. On each tarry blob Eric pressed something from the forest floor – moss, leaves, bark, and so on.

Making me look invisible seemed to take everyone's mind off our problems – for the moment, anyway.

"You look terrific," Eric beamed. "Even if they stare right at you, they won't see you."

We'd found a tree that had been struck by lightning, and both Eric and Anna used the charred wood to plaster my face with black soot. "I'm just glad it's warm out tonight," I said.

"Yes," Anna agreed, painting my ears black, "last

night was much cooler."

"They probably won't be expecting us to backtrack and sneak up on them," Eric said. "But you'd still better be super careful and –"

"– I know that," I snapped, and then grimaced when I heard my harsh voice. The idea of any of us being stuck here forever was getting to me. I took a deep breath and added, "But if I'm not back by morning, you and Anna better leave without me during tomorrow's solstice. There's no point in all four of us being stuck here."

Anna and Eric looked at each other. "We'll see," Eric said. He gave me his pocketknife and the zapper and I shoved both weapons deep in my pocket. I felt a lot better knowing I was armed and dangerous – okay, maybe I wasn't *dangerous*, but at least I was *armed*. I took off my wristwatch and jammed that into my pants too. I didn't want the luminous dial attracting attention. Like I said, I was going to be careful.

"Does that clock have an alarm?" Anna asked, pointing at my pants.

"'Clock'?" I said. "Huh?"

"Will it beep every hour?"

I laughed. "Oh, I see. No, my watch doesn't do anything fancy, it's just waterproof."

The only other thing I took with me was one of the walkie-talkies. I slid it into my zippered pocket – thank goodness for cargo pants – and said, "Remember, the radio is for emergency use by me only. Don't call me no matter what, or you'll give away my position for sure."

"Yeah, yeah," Eric said. "Don't call you, you'll call me. Got it."

I drank half a bottle of water and made my way down to the river. The moon wasn't above the trees yet, but I was still able to make good time in the darkness. When I got close to the spot where the highway bridge in Sultana would eventually be, I climbed the bank and entered the forest.

I stuck to the open areas, slowly and quietly winding my way toward the fork in the river. With each step I pressed down lightly to minimize the crunch of leaves and twigs. And when I thought my footfall was too loud, I paused and waited nervously for warning shouts. After thirty minutes I began to catch the faint smell of wood smoke. I stopped again. *Was it good or bad that I could smell their fire?* The little hairs on the back of my neck tingled and sprang to attention.

I closed my eyes and tried to concentrate. *Think, Cody, think.* What was it we learned in Boy Scouts?

That's right, I thought as I remembered. If you're trying to sneak up on an animal, you *wanted* to have the wind in your face, so that the animal couldn't smell you. I allowed myself a quick grin. There was no wind – only a slight breeze – but the smoke I could smell meant I *was* downwind *and* moving in the right direction. *Perfect.*

The nearly full moon rose higher as I prowled ever closer. With each pace I gave myself more time to wait, listen, and plan my next step. Suddenly, a wave of laughter reached my ears. The camp was close.

I took a cautious step, and listened. Crickets and other insects buzzed softly around me, and I was sure the bats were out now too. Their eerie black bodies flew in sloppy circles around the canopy as they munched on mosquitoes and other night insects.

I took another ten slow steps, and listened some more. I could recognize different voices now, though the bugs were still competing for my attention.

WAIT! What was that?

I was so busy trying to angle my ears closer, I almost lost track of my other senses. That was when I caught a slight movement near a tree, thirty steps ahead. I froze, sank to a crouch, and waited. Staring at the spot, I urged my eyes to focus. But there was nothing visible in the shadowy night. *Had I imagined it?* I willed my ears to listen even harder, but heard no noise. Still, I didn't dare move. I had seen enough movies where someone gave away their position by being impatient and moving too soon. I wasn't about to make that blunder. We had way too much at stake!

If someone was there, they'd be patient too. So I waited, listened, and watched.

Fifteen minutes went by and my legs had cramped. It felt like *nearly* enough time had passed, but *nearly* wasn't good enough, so I stayed frozen. I trusted my eyes and my instincts – because I *had* seen something.

The tree I was staring at suddenly came to life. Only it *wasn't* a tree! It was a man cloaked in fur, and he had been squatting near the ground. He stood up and grunted something in a language I didn't understand to a second person only three feet away. I watched as they both moved like ghosts toward their camp.

That was way too close. I had almost walked smack into two lookouts. Thank goodness for my camouflage.

That was my first close call. The second one happened twenty minutes later.

After the sentries left, I prowled around the perimeter of the camp on my knees. I watched the camp carefully for signs of Rachel – and then another man walked out of a tent and headed straight toward me.

For a moment, I wavered between fleeing and holding my ground. If I ran, he would for sure see me, and then I would have the whole tribe after me. But if I held my ground, he might walk straight into me.

I had to take that chance, and trust my disguise would hide me. But that didn't slow my heartbeat one bit.

When he was five feet away, he stopped and began to pee. I closed my eyes so he couldn't see their whites glowing in the moonlight. I cringed at the sound of liquid hitting the soil. Holding my breath, I avoided the impulse to cry "P-U!". When I finally heard him turn and walk away, I opened my eyes again. *This was nuts!*

The camp was smaller than I'd imagined. There were seven teepee tents set up to form roughly the shape of a half-circle. Even in the moonlight I could see that each tent was elaborately decorated with paintings.

Beyond the tents I saw the final proof I was looking for. The Red and MacFie Rivers were right where they were supposed to be – just like in *our* Sultana. The riverbank in the distance was lined with several birch bark canoes. A cooking fire burned near the middle of the camp.

I couldn't see Rachel among the adults and children. Except – the second tent from the river had a guard posted near the front opening. Maybe Rachel was in there?

I crawled into a thicket of brush, and settled in to observe the camp.

I couldn't see anything sinister or warlike about the group. Women chatted quietly around the fire – some were rocking infants. A few older kids were gathered around an elder, like they were listening to a story. And many others were going to bed or already asleep. The whole scene looked pretty peaceful.

But they had Rachel and we wanted her back.

The tent flap opened on the second teepee. I held my breath. Rachel emerged from the shelter followed by a man who was probably a foot taller than me. The tall guy said something to an old lady who had been poking the fire. She stopped what she was doing and led Rachel into the forest. Rachel obediently followed, and they both returned five minutes later.

Rachel wasn't tied up. In fact, despite the fact she was being watched by the tall guy – and probably by everyone else in the camp – she looked at ease. I was relieved to see that she was healthy and alert. She walked to the fire and hovered around it. Some of the other women came to talk to her and offered her food or water, but Rachel declined with a shake of her head. She often looked up at the sky or around the camp.

Anna told us that Rachel was unconscious when they carried her away, which I guess explained why Rachel didn't just run into the forest as fast as she could – she had no idea where she was or where she had landed. And since she didn't even know we were here with her, it made a lot of sense for her to stay with the tribe.

I desperately wanted to scream, "We're here, Rachel! Don't worry, we'll rescue you!" But of course, I kept my mouth shut. *Poor Rachel.*

How the heck could we get her away from them? Would they just let her leave? Could we trade something for her? But what could we offer them?

I looked around the camp for anything that might help us rescue Rachel. Thanks to the stars, the moon, and the flames from the fire, I had a great view of the people near the campfire. But there was something about that tall man – the one who had followed Rachel out of the tent – that grabbed my attention. He just *looked* different from the others around him.

I squinted through the night at the stranger. I wished I'd brought the binoculars with me so I could really zoom in on his features. He was close enough that I could see he had dark hair like the others, but a longer nose, paler skin, and a bigger head. Then he turned so that the fire illuminated the right side of his face, and I saw all I needed to see.

An Egyptian tattoo!

I didn't know what the giant bug on his neck symbolized, but I knew from all the research we had done for our plaque that it had to be Egyptian. It definitely didn't match the customs of the Woodland Cree – the tribe I suspected the people here belonged to. In fact, I doubted there even *were* beetles like that in Canada. We learned in school that the Cree tattooed each other with artistic designs and patterns, but this looked too *neat*. There was no way a guy with a tattoo like that was from around here. He had to be from the future – from Egypt.

As I lay hidden, I began thinking about what Aubey had tried to tell Eric just before we disappeared at the stones. I was so distracted, Aubey's warning had barely registered in my brain. But now – now I wished I hadn't been so quick to cut him off. Because there was something about this guy ... something we were supposed to know ...

It doesn't matter, I decided, shaking my head. I knew this man had to be from the future, and that little piece of information was enough to form a rescue plan. I fine-tuned my scheme in my head while I waited for the camp to shut down for the night. One hour later, as the two lookouts made a final sweep of the perimeter and turned in for the night, I felt confident we could get Rachel and return home.

I gave them another fifteen minutes to zonk out and then I slid into their camp. Tiptoeing between two tents, I went straight to a dead poplar tree near the center of their encampment. It had a million holes in it from woodpeckers or squirrels trying to use its remains.

I dug my portable communicator from my pocket and carefully turned it on. I was terrified it would let out an electronic squawk, but it didn't. So far, so good. Reaching as high as I could, I placed the receiver in a knot hole and covered the opening with a thin layer of moss.

I left the camp as cautiously as I had entered it. When I was sure I was out of earshot of anyone in the tents, I picked up the pace and jogged to the MacFie. I hid in the bush there for twenty minutes to be certain I wasn't being followed. I didn't want to be the dummy that let us *all* get captured.

After I caught my breath again, I ran down to the river and then south to Anna and Eric.

"Pssst!" I whispered, when I got near the spot where I had left them. "Eric? Anna?"

"What took you so long?" Eric said, stepping from behind a spruce tree. "I was starting to think you got lost." He led me another hundred feet into the forest, where he and Anna had made a small fire. Anna was asleep under a thin, silver thermal blanket. She was using a backpack as a pillow.

After two sleepless nights in the bush, Anna deserved some rest. We could brief her in the morning.

"They have her," I said quietly to Eric.

He sighed and placed another stick in the fire. "Tell me everything."

He listened intently while I recounted my close calls. He laughed when I explained that my disguise was so good that I had almost been peed on. And his eyes grew huge when I told him that an Egyptian man might be living among the tribe. I finished by saying, "I think they're Woodland Cree."

Eric nodded. "Teepees?"

"Yeah." We had learned in history class that the Ojibwe lived in domed lodges called wigwams, while the Cree preferred to live in teepees.

"So," he said, "do you have any ideas for getting Rachel back?"

I grinned. "Yeah, actually I do. But it's such a long shot we should have a Plan B too – just in case."

I told Eric how I stashed the other communicator in the tree and what I wanted to do tomorrow.

"If that's Plan A," he shook his head, "we'll definitely need a backup."

We made ourselves comfortable around the fire and tried to get some sleep. But as exhausted as we were, I don't think either one of us slept very much. We had way too much at stake. The rest of our lives would be determined by what happened in the morning. If we didn't rescue Rachel, and if we didn't all make it back to the stones by high noon, we'd be stuck here for a long time, maybe forever.

I woke up sweating. The sun had managed to find a gap in the trees and it was blasting my face with heat. I sat up, rubbed my eyes, and wiped my grimy forehead.

"Good morning," Anna said. She must have just returned from the river. Her face was clean and some of her brown hair was still wet.

I shook Eric awake and we trundled down to the river to wash ourselves. Only it took me a lot longer to scrub away all the soot and junk I had applied to my skin the night before. But all the rubbing and cleaning sure woke me up.

When I returned to the bush, I filled Anna in on everything I had seen last night.

"I am glad Rachel's safe and close by," she said with visible relief. She still felt responsible for not being able to save Rachel. "But how are we going to rescue her?"

"Just before Eric and I entered the wormhole at Mit Rahina, we were told by our friend, Aubey, that there might be another person here from our time."

Anna said, "So ... we have a contact in the camp?"

I wasn't sure if that's what Aubey had been trying to tell me in the seconds before we vanished. But what else could he have meant? I had been so preoccupied with getting the satellite phone to Eric, I never did hear everything he was saying.

"Tell her about the Egyptian man," Eric said. "Tell

her why you think you saw *him*."

"Oh, yeah," I said. "The tallest guy in the camp doesn't look like a Cree –"

"– I saw a tall man too," Anna said excitedly, "but I couldn't see his face."

"*And*," I went on, "he has a giant tattoo on his neck. I saw it last night. The tattoo looked Egyptian-ish and I'm sure I saw that style of bug in Rachel's books or on one of those hieroglyphic web sites."

"What did it look like?" Anna asked. "Describe it."

"Well," I said, "it looked like a bug – a beetle. And it was as big as my whole hand!"

Anna grabbed a blackened stick from the fire and quickly drew a bug on the bark of a nearby poplar tree. "Did it look like this?"

"It was far away," I admitted, "but, yeah. It looked pretty much like that. Why?"

Anna smiled. "That is the sacred scarab. It represents *Khepri* – he's the Egyptian sun god in the morning. He *must* be from Egypt. No one here would have a tattoo of a scarab."

"Great!" I said. "I thought he might be, but it's nice to have confirmation."

"Yeah, yeah," Eric said impatiently. "Now tell her about your plan."

"Last night I hid one of our walkie-talkies in a tree, inside their camp, and today I want to walk into their camp and ask for Rachel's return. If they refuse, Eric is going to use his walkie-talkie to trick them into thinking the tree is talking to them."

"A talking tree?" Anna said. "Why a tree?"

"It doesn't matter *what* is talking," I explained. "We learned in school that the Cree have a strong bond with nature. They believe that everything in the natural world has a spirit, and that all spirits have to be respected. If we can convince them that the spirit of the trees is asking for Rachel's release, then –"

Anna held up her hand to stop me. "But you don't know how to speak the Cree language."

"That's where you come in," Eric said.

"Your dad told us you're great with languages," I said. "Is your Arabic as good as your English?"

Anna grinned. "My Arabic is even better. My mother is Egyptian and when I'm with her, I only speak Arabic."

"Good," I said. "Because we'll need you to communicate with Mr. Tattoo in Arabic, and then he can translate into Cree."

Eric chuckled. "'Mr. Tattoo,' eh? I like that."

Anna ignored Eric. "But I wonder if he still speaks Arabic?"

"I sure hope so," Eric said, chewing on a granola bar. "That's a critical part of our plan."

Eric and I slung our bags on our backs and we all headed north toward Rachel and the Cree. "And remember," I said to Eric, "when we get close, stay way back. It's probably best if you approach from the west and then hide. There are a couple of good spots in that area, where you should be able to see everything, *and* still hear me when I yell."

"No problem," he said.

"And don't say anything until I tell you to."

Eric nodded and began walking north.

When we were five minutes from their camp, Eric left Anna and me and headed west, to approach the camp from the far side. We gave him fifteen minutes to get in position. Then Anna and I did the unthinkable: we walked straight into the camp, in the daylight, with no disguise, to save Rachel.

CHAPTER 8

The Cree were so unprepared for our arrival, they didn't know how to react. A few people working around the fire simply froze and stared at us.

I put my bag down at the base of the old poplar tree and yelled, "HELLO!"

A second later, Anna yelled, "*MARHABBAH!* HELLO!"

We had everyone's attention now. People came running from all directions. Tent flaps opened and people poured out and surrounded us. Some of the men grabbed spears and formed a sloppy circle around Anna and me. Kids who had been playing in the water came running to see the pale-skinned strangers, but hid behind mothers and grandmothers and great-grandmothers.

"Cody!" Rachel bullied her way through the crowd and ran up to me, her face full of relief. "I knew you would come for me! I knew it!" She gave me such a tight hug, I thought I felt my rib cage creak. "And happy birthday."

"Thanks," I whispered. I had completely forgotten I had turned thirteen today. "Eric's with me too, but don't look around for him – he's hiding in the forest."

Rachel released me and stared for a second at Anna

with a confused look. But then her eyes brightened – she must've figured out Anna was the one who the German scientists had sent us to rescue. She gave Anna a quick hug too, and I heard Rachel say, "I'm glad you're safe."

A grumpy looking guy – probably the Chief – pulled Rachel back and barked something at us in Cree.

Anna ignored him and yelled again. "*MARHABBAH!*"

Mr. Tattoo pushed his way forward and stared at Anna. He looked about forty years old, and he kept his black hair cut short, unlike the rest of the Cree men. From up close, the scarab on his neck looked pretty scary. The bug tattoo was all black, but it was done so well, it looked like it was actually sitting on his neck. He stopped in front of Anna and me and glared down at us.

Anna asked him something in Arabic, and he quickly responded in the same language.

"His Arabic's perfect," Anna said.

So far, so good, I thought.

"Tell him that we're from the twenty-first century, and that we came here from Egypt," I said to Anna. "Tell him we need his help urgently."

I watched Mr. Tattoo's face as Anna translated what I said into Arabic. At first, he frowned, but then he nodded and a smile spread across his face. It looked a little sinister, but then again, some people smiled that way.

The Chief started getting twitchy and yelled at us for a second time in Cree. I don't think he liked not knowing what was going on.

"Tell Mr. Tattoo," I said, "to tell the Chief that we have come for Rachel."

I waited for Anna to tell Mr. Tattoo and for Mr. Tattoo to tell the Chief.

The Chief looked at us and then at his people. And then he laughed. In fact, he laughed so hard it became contagious and soon everyone was creased up and laughing at us. The only people that weren't laughing were Anna, Rachel, Mr. Tattoo, and me.

This was going to be harder than I thought.

When the laughter subsided, I turned to Anna. "Tell Mr. Tattoo to tell the Chief that the spirits demand Rachel's return. Or his people will be punished."

The Chief listened to Mr. Tattoo's translation and then said something in Cree.

Anna turned to me. "The Chief wants to know *what* specific spirit are you talking about?"

Fine, I thought. It was time for some twenty-first century magic.

I spun around and pointed at the old tree. As loud as I could I yelled, "Okay, Eric, start saying something. And you better make it good!"

The radio transmitter I hid in the tree the night before came to life. *"Hi Rachel,"* the tree said. *"Don't worry about anything. I know this looks like a goofy plan, but it should work."*

A collective murmur rose around us. Rachel looked at me and then the tree dubiously. Clearly, she wasn't convinced our plan was going to work.

When the tree – I mean, Eric – stopped talking, I said to Anna, "Tell him we can talk to *all* the spirits, and they *all* want Rachel to leave with us."

Anna translated for Mr. Tattoo who translated for the Chief. He considered our words but shook his head again. He said something to Mr. Tattoo, who repeated everything to Anna, who repeated everything to me. It was like a really bad game of telephone. And then I realized that the telephone game didn't exist yet – so it was like we had just invented it for the first time.

I shook my head and returned to the matter at hand. Anna was translating. "The Chief said that Sutekh – that's his Egyptian name – was a gift for his people from the spirit world, and the spirit world has now blessed him with another gift, Rachel. He says the spirits cannot have her back."

Some of the kids grew bored with all the talking and drifted back to the water for a swim.

I turned back to the tree and yelled. "They don't believe us, Eric! Say something else and try to sound like you're mad!"

The tree spoke again, angrily. *"Listen up, you bozos! I want my sister back now. I like her – sometimes I even love her, but not very often – and I want her back!"*

Rachel let out a soft moan and covered her eyes. One of the older ladies standing next to her rubbed her back as if to comfort her.

The Chief glared at the tree until an old man

whispered something in his ear. The Chief nodded, cupped his hands together and blew into the space between his thumbs. The eerie call of a loon sounded from his hands. He then yelled across the river in Cree.

Sutekh spoke to Anna, and Anna repeated what he said in English. "The Chief has called upon his personal spirit for a sign."

At first, we heard nothing, and I started to feel relieved. Maybe our plan could still work.

But then –

WHOOO-OOO-HOOOOOO. The distinct cry of a loon echoed across the water.

That's great. That's just great, I thought.

The Chief, of course, looked pretty smug. He said something to his people and murmurs of agreement rose around him.

I could imagine what he said too: "This kid can talk to the tree spirits, but I can talk to the animal spirits."

The tree behind me decided to speak again. *"Okay, Cody,"* Eric said through the tree. *"From where I'm hiding it doesn't look like this is working. Let's go to Plan B."*

The warrior-types in the band had already realized we weren't a threat and put down their spears and bows. Sure, we were strange – and probably a huge nuisance – but it was obvious we couldn't hurt them.

I pulled my digital camera from my pocket and turned it on. The tribesmen who were still hanging around leaned in to look when the lens opened up and expanded outward. I scrolled back through the pictures

I had taken and found the one I wanted – Rachel by *The Lion of Nubia*. I zoomed in on Rachel so that her head filled the small LCD display.

"LOOK!" I screamed, holding up the camera so that everyone could see Rachel on the monitor. "Her spirit remains in another world. She is not complete with your people. We *must* take her back!"

Anna quickly translated and Sutekh followed suit. The Chief rubbed his chin thoughtfully and then picked his teeth with one of the many claws strung around his neck. I held my breath while he considered the facts.

After several excruciating minutes the Chief stuck out his hand. I passed him the camera and let him look at Rachel's "trapped" spirit. He felt the weight of the camera and turned it over and over in his leathery palm.

Without warning, he placed it on a rock and smashed it with another stone. *CRUNCH!*

"HEY," I screamed. "That was my birthday present!"

The Chief spoke, and Sutekh and Anna translated. "He said that the spirit of Rachel is now free."

The tree piped up again. *"That didn't look good at all,"* Eric said. *"Do we have a Plan C?"* But the talking tree didn't impress anyone anymore, and no one even looked at it.

The Chief made a final decisive speech which Anna said went something like this: "You are all here as rewards from the spirit world. You will stay with us as our family. And we will welcome you as we have

Gift-From-The-Stones." Apparently that's what they called Sutekh.

The Chief and all the other Cree turned their backs to us and resumed doing whatever they were doing before we showed up. Sutekh stayed with the three of us by the dead tree.

I groaned. So much for my plans – both A *and* B.

And just when I thought things couldn't get any worse, things got worse – a lot worse.

Sutekh walked up to the tree, stared at it for a minute, and then reached into the hole and pulled out my walkie-talkie. He switched it off and passed it back to me. "Who sent you here?" Sutekh asked in near-perfect English.

"What?" I asked. I was so shocked, I had to remember to close my mouth after I finished talking.

"You speak English?" Rachel said, equally astonished. "Why didn't you tell me earlier?"

"Was it Egyptian Antiquities Limited?" Sutekh ignored her. "Did EAL send you here?"

"What?" I repeated, then shook my head. "No! We came here to bring Anna and Rachel back. That's all."

Sutekh didn't look convinced. "I don't believe you. How do I know EAL didn't send you to bring *me* back?"

We stared up at Sutekh like he was nuts.

"Look," Rachel said, "we just want to go back – back to our time. Anna and I *accidentally* fell into the wormhole, and Cody and Eric came to bring us back."

Anna nodded. "That's the truth. If *you* want to stay

here, we won't stop you."

"Yeah," I said, "but we need to get out of here. If you can convince them to let us go, you'd be doing us a huge favor."

Sutekh didn't say anything, and we stood there, as if holding our breath. The only noise that reached us was the kids swimming and laughing in the river, around the bend.

Sutekh sighed. "I'm sorry," he said, finally. "I wasn't sure I could trust you at first. I'm still afraid that EAL – well, anyway, that's in the past. Or the future, to be more precise."

"But why on Earth *wouldn't* you trust us?" Rachel asked, incredulous. She still sounded annoyed that Sutekh had hidden from her that he could speak English. "What are you afraid of?"

"We only want to go home," Anna added.

Sutekh sighed. "I live in fear every day that EAL will send someone to punish me, to bring me back, or worse – to kill me."

I raised my eyebrows. Maybe he really was cuckoo. Maybe that's what Aubey was trying to tell Eric. "Why the heck would EAL want to punish you?" I asked.

"Thirteen years ago – I was twenty-six then – EAL asked me to go through the stones and return with information – where had I landed, what time period did I travel to, and so on. They knew it would be very dangerous, so I was paid an enormous amount of money for the risk I would be taking. But as soon as I met the Cree, I decided to stay instead. This is what I always wanted –" Sutekh waved his arms around the camp "– to live with nature and a peaceful people."

"But you could have left?" Rachel asked.

"Yes," Sutekh said, "but I didn't want to leave. I *wanted* to stay."

"So why didn't you tell the Chief to let *us* leave?" I asked.

"As I said, I had to discover the real *reason* you came here. I needed to know that you weren't here for me."

"Please trust us," Anna pleaded, "we only want to go home. But if the Chief won't let us go, we'll miss our chance to go back. Will you help us?"

Sutekh looked down his nose at each of us. "I will go and speak with the Chief. Stay near the camp or ... or the Chief won't be happy." He turned around and left us to go search for the Chief, who must have returned to his tent, because I couldn't see him anywhere.

When Sutekh was gone, Rachel said, "I don't trust that guy."

"Yeah," I admitted, "that's a wacky explanation. But is it any more bizarre than everything else that's happened? At least he's offered to help us now."

Rachel didn't look convinced. "He spent a long time pretending he couldn't speak English – enough time to learn everything he could. And we don't even know what he told the Chief when he was translating."

"Well, his name is sort of fitting – *Sutekh*." Anna

said it like it left a bad taste on her tongue.

"Why's that?" I asked.

"It is a common Egyptian boy's name now," Anna said. "But in ancient times, Sutekh was the evil god of chaos."

I considered that as I watched Sutekh disappear inside a teepee. "We just have to be careful. For now, we *pretend* we trust him, and hope he can help us." I looked over the camp, which had returned to its usual rhythm. "We can't make a run for it anymore, not with everyone watching. We need a plan, and we need it fast."

CHAPTER 9

I left Anna and Rachel by the dead tree, and tried to look as casual as possible as I snuck off to find Eric. I figured if I pretended I had to go to the washroom, no one would become suspicious. I could have used the walkie-talkie to call him, but after seeing what the Chief had done to my camera, I didn't want to risk losing that too. Plus, we should save the batteries.

The entire time I was walking away, I forced myself *not* to run, but believe me, I wanted to grab Eric and the girls and race straight for the pillars.

I knew the general area where Eric might have hid, so I headed toward the higher land west of camp. The elevated landforms there would've provided a perfect spot for him to see the whole site. But when I got to the first granite outcrop, he wasn't there.

I looked around and saw another potential hideout. It was farther from the camp and closer to the Red River, but it was even higher. I turned around to face the camp, to test Eric's vantage point. Yup, from here I could see the whole camp, and even without the binoculars, I could see Rachel and Anna standing by the tree. With the binoculars, Eric would have had a terrific view. But when I moved closer, I frowned.

Crud! He wasn't there either. *Come on, Eric, where*

are you?

I started to take my walkie-talkie from my pants pocket when I heard a muffled noise coming from down by the river.

Eric?

I fought my way through the scratchy shrubs to get down to the bank.

"Thank God!" Eric cried. "What took you so long?"

It took me a few seconds to understand what I was seeing. Eric was on his knees next to an unconscious girl, and desperately trying to revive her. A boy and another girl stood by nervously, whimpering and mumbling in Cree. All three kids looked like they were about six or seven years old.

"They were swimming," Eric said, while performing quick compressions on her little chest with one hand. "Something must have happened ... they started screaming for help ..." He gave me a desperate look. "I *had* to help. She's not breathing ... and ... I can't feel a pulse!"

"No pulse?" I mumbled.

Eric nodded and switched hands. "But check yourself," he said. "Maybe I just couldn't find it."

I dropped to my knees across from Eric, on the other side of the girl. I rechecked all the heartbeat pulse points we had learned about in our school CPR class – neck, wrist, and ankle – but didn't feel anything. But that could mean nothing: maybe I just couldn't hear it.

Eric was soaked with sweat. "Here," I said, "let

me take over. Take a break." I gently pinched her tiny nose like we were taught in Health class and blew twice into her mouth. Her lips were cold too and I wondered how long she had been under water. *Oh no! Was she already dead?*

I shook my head and took a deep breath. I couldn't panic now – her life depended on us staying calm. I pushed down on her small chest with another thirty quick compressions. *Push hard, push fast. Push hard, push fast.* Our instructor's chant kept going through my head. I also remembered his warning that it wasn't uncommon to crack ribs while performing CPR. That didn't make me feel any better. *Push hard, push fast.*

No response.

"I tried calling you on the walkie-talkie," Eric said, huffing and puffing to catch his breath, "but ..."

"Yeah," I mumbled, "Sutekh turned it off." I repeated the resuscitation steps over and over and over – until I was exhausted too – but she still wasn't breathing.

Eric nudged me aside and took over again.

The girl was turning blue and I was getting frantic. I had never seen anyone die before, and I realized now how awful it was to watch life drift away, especially from someone so helpless and young. We *had* to save her.

While Eric puffed away, and the other kids began to cry, I held my head in my hands. And then I had an idea.

Desperately, I groped through Eric's backpack looking for the zapper. I wasn't sure if it could revive a heart, but it was all we had left to try now.

Eric stopped working on the girl and stared at the zapper I was holding.

"Should we?" I asked, turning it over and over in my sweaty hands.

Eric nodded and pulled his hand away from her body. "We have to try *something*, Cody. She's ... dying ... dead." He choked on the last word.

I touched the probe to the center of her heart and pressed the trigger.

ZAP!

The girl's friends jumped back, terrified.

Her tiny body twitched violently and then went limp. Eric leaned over her and continued performing CPR, but she still didn't respond.

"Try it again," Eric gasped.

There were no settings or adjustments on the device, so there was nothing I could do to alter the charge. But if it could stun an adult, I reasoned, it should be ... just ... enough to ...

This time I pressed the metal tip to the left side of her chest. I hoped there was *some* truth to all the crazy stuff I saw on TV.

ZAP!

Her little chest jerked up and fell back. And then – was I seeing things? – it rose and fell again, by itself. She was alive!

Eric rolled her over onto her side. "Oh man. It worked. She's *breathing*." Our patient coughed and gagged, trying to clear her waterlogged lungs.

The two kids waiting next to us stared in wonder. Then, they jumped up and down, hugging each other and laughing.

We watched, fascinated, as the girl who had been so close to death recovered her color and warmed up quickly under the sun. She continued coughing for a while but she seemed to be out of danger now.

We sat with the little girl and her friends and waited for her to recover fully. She sat up after twenty minutes and began speaking to her companions. I thought it might be best if they didn't tell anyone what happened – or they'd start asking questions about the zapper – so I put my finger up to my lips and went "Shhh." I wasn't sure if that worked as a timeless indicator of *keep quiet*, but it was worth a try.

The kids looked at each other and then back at us. One of them shrugged.

Eric tried next. He pointed to the camp, and then used his hand to mimic a talking gesture – a mouth opening and closing. He shook his head with a stern look on his face, emphasizing that this would be a bad thing to do.

The boy pointed toward the camp, nodded, and then repeated my "Shhh" gesture. I suppose even kids in the past knew to keep secrets from parents and adults. Our victim coughed up some more water, smiled, and held her finger to her lips. I think the only thing that kept her from saying "Shhh" was her tired throat.

Good. We were all on the same page now.

Eric and I followed the children back to the camp. The girl we revived stopped every twenty feet for a good fit of coughing, but she seemed to be in good spirits. Eric had tried to carry her – thinking she might be too weak to stand – but she squirmed away, eager to walk with her friends. I guess she had enough attention for one morning. The slow trip back allowed plenty of time for me to fill Eric in on what happened at the tree.

"Are you serious?" Eric asked. "Sutekh *wants* to be here?"

I nodded. "And now he's talking to the Chief to see if we can leave. But we can't trust him," I whispered. "He might be hiding something else. So we have to be careful when he's near."

"I guess so," Eric said, looking around for Sutekh. I realized that Eric still hadn't met him or seen what he looked like.

Rachel ran over to us as soon as we entered the camp. "Gosh," she said, "what took you two so long? We were getting worried."

"It's a long story," Eric said, grinning, "and I'll tell you about it later. But we're both heroes."

Rachel looked at her bother with confusion. "What are you talking –?"

"– CHILDREN!" Sutekh waved us over to one of the tents. "COME HERE."

"This better be good news," I said. "We're running out of time."

We all glanced nervously at the sun as we headed toward the teepee.

Sutekh glared at Eric and then scowled at me, but he didn't question my lengthy absence from camp. He held back the tent flap and we all piled into the Chief's home. The Chief, a few women, and a bunch of other senior members were already sitting around in a circle. They left a gap in the circle and Sutekh ordered us to sit there. The tent was smoky, hot, and packed with people.

When everyone had settled in, the Chief started things off with a long speech. My hands were sweating fiercely, and I tried hard to keep them from shaking as I listened. We had no idea what Sutekh may have told the Chief. I was worried we had made a mistake trusting him – instead of making a run for it – *and* I sensed that the sun was rapidly reaching its highest point in the sky. We needed to be on our way to the pillars to make the solstice deadline and we didn't have time for any more shenanigans or complications from the Chief.

Finally, he stopped talking and Sutekh summarized his lecture for us in English. "The Chief has reconsidered. He does not understand why the spirits would want such pale, sick-looking children back. You are all welcome to stay here forever, but the Chief will leave the final decision to the spirit of the stones."

"What does that mean?" I asked.

"It means," Sutekh said, "that if you can all pass

through the pillars, the spirits *must* want you back. And that is fine with the Chief. But if you fail to travel back to your world, the Chief will take that as a sign from the spirits that they *don't* want you and you must stay."

I couldn't believe it. That was *exactly* what we wanted! "That sounds reasonable," I said, struggling to keep my voice even.

"And if you leave," Sutekh continued, "he wants you to tell the spirits to *stop* sending him troublesome gifts."

I exchanged glances with Eric. There was no way we could guarantee that, but we could warn the scientists and Aubey when we returned. "Sure," Eric said, "whatever."

I felt that I should show my appreciation, so I said, "Tell the Chief we thank him, and we will ask all the spirits to bless him and his people with excellent hunting, fishing, and health."

I stood up hoping that would signal an end to the meeting. But it didn't.

The Chief pointed at the ground, the universal sign for *Sit your butt back down*. So I sat my butt back down. He solemnly spoke to me and I waited to find out what he'd said from Sutekh.

"The Chief said that you should show your gratitude immediately by presenting him with a gift."

Eric groaned. "What a guy."

I rolled my eyes. Secretly, I thought Eric and the Chief were a lot alike.

I reached into my pocket and pulled out the folding pocketknife Rudi had bought for Eric. We hadn't used it for anything yet so the blade still sparkled like new. As soon as I flipped out a blade, the Cree "Ahhh'd," appreciating the knife's shininess. I folded and unfolded it several times, so everyone could admire the craftsmanship. Then I flicked open the steel a final time, picked up a piece of firewood, and shaved off a foot-long curl of wood.

The Chief laughed and clapped his hands together like it was his birthday. He snatched the knife from my hand as I was tucking the blade away and it accidentally sliced his thumb open. He grinned and proudly showed the group the blood flowing down his hand.

I guess he liked it.

"I still can't believe that guy," Eric complained as we headed down the trail toward the pillars.

"Let it go," Rachel said.

But he wouldn't. "He kidnaps you, he smashes Cody's camera, and then he has the nerve to demand a gift – *my* knife."

"As long as we don't miss the solstice," I said, looking up and studying the position of the sun, "I don't care what he takes from us."

"They should have had a massive feast for us – like in the movies. Why couldn't they make a huge fire and barbeque steaks and hamburgers and chicken wings and ...?"

"– I don't think they have any of those foods," Anna interrupted.

"Well, they could have tried," Eric whined. "Everyone knows how to make a burger."

Anna laughed and said, "Maybe you are right, Eric. The bun could be made from the bannock bread, and if they mashed up deer meat they could form meat patties."

Eric laughed. "It's not a Big Mac, but I don't feel super picky right now."

I was pretty sure we would make it to the pillars on time, but we all hustled down the trail at a near-run anyway. Sutekh was the only one from the Cree camp accompanying the four of us. The Chief wasn't into emotional farewells – thank goodness. He simply waved us away with a flick of his fingers.

Sutekh led the way through the forest. I felt a bit bad for not trusting him, but we weren't out of the woods yet – literally. Anything could still happen. We let Sutekh get far enough ahead of us that he couldn't hear us. Then I did our best to fill Rachel in on everything that had happened since she disappeared at Mit Rahina.

When I finished, Rachel said, "So during a summer solstice, when all those planets line up behind the sun, a wormhole opens up."

"Yes, exactly," I said, stepping over a fallen oak

tree. "Anna's dad told us that the planetary alignment is kind of like the tumblers inside a huge safe. When all the planets click into place at the same time, the timeline of history bends and touches, and a shortcut to the past opens up. Sort of like the doors on a vault."

Anna looked back over her shoulder and added, "And that only happens every thirteen years."

Rachel nodded. "So the ancient people that painted and carved those symbols and messages on the stones were marking the exact location of the wormhole where the shortcut would appear."

"It was just rotten luck," I said, "that Anna, and then you, were standing in that spot during the solstice, when the cosmic alignment occurred."

Sutekh turned around and pointed ahead, down the trail.

We were back at the pillars.

There was so much happening when we arrived the day before, I never really had a chance to examine the markers. These ones were made of a darker stone than those in Egypt – probably granite. The size and shape, however, was exactly the same – as thick as a car tire, chest high, and topped with a wider, flat piece of stone. Each column was covered with crazy messages and glyphs.

"The sun has not yet reached its highest point," Sutekh said. "You have three or four minutes before the sun will stand still."

Thank goodness. We made it, I thought.

Eric went straight to the center of the three stones and threw down his bag. "Good. So who wants to go first?"

"Ladies first?" I asked Rachel, tossing my backpack on the ground next to Eric's. I dug out a water bottle and passed it around.

"Do you think it could carry all of us at once?" Eric said. "Or are we too heavy?"

Anna took a drink of water and gave the bottle to Eric. "I don't think it works like an elevator," she said wryly.

Eric frowned. "I'm just worried that the solstice won't last long enough to transport all of us."

"Yeah, you've got a point," I agreed. "But we do know that two people can pass through the wormhole at the same time. So why don't Anna and Rachel go first, and then we'll jump in as soon as they vanish."

Anna and Rachel nodded. It seemed like a good plan. The girls stood in the center with their arms around each other – and waited to disappear.

Eric paced in a circle around the girls. "It should happen any second now."

Anna and Rachel shook with nervous energy and hugged each other close.

I picked up my pack and swung it on my back again. "We'll see you on the other side," I said, trying hard to sound optimistic.

Eric strapped his bag on too. "Any second now ..."

"Stop saying that." Rachel snapped. "I'm nervous

enough already."

Many seconds passed, but nothing happened.

Eric stopped doing laps around Anna and Rachel. "Something's not right," he mumbled.

"Give it time," I said. "Don't move now. Stay put." But even as I said that, I wondered if Eric was right.

"Why are we still here?" Rachel asked, staring angrily at the sky.

We didn't know the answer to that, so we didn't say anything.

The sun was exactly where it was supposed to be. If we waited any longer –

Sutekh, who had been standing several feet back from the center of the pillars, shook his head. "The sun no longer stands still," he said, sounding smug. "It is moving again toward the west."

"But how could that be?" I asked. "We were *definitely* here before the solstice started."

Anna and Rachel refused to give up and stubbornly stayed in the center of the stones.

Eric unsnapped his pack and threw it on the grass. "So now what?" he griped, to nobody in particular. "Are we stuck here forever?"

"This is crazy," I said. "We did everything right. We're doing the same thing we did to get here, and it should have worked."

"Unless we've already missed the summer solstice," Anna said, letting go of Rachel and moving away from her. "Perhaps the days are already growing shorter here – here in the past."

Rachel looked stricken. "What does that mean? You mean we'll have to wait until next year's solstice to go home?"

Eric and I looked at each other.

"No," Eric said. "Remember, we can only use the wormhole during the astrological alignment that occurs on your thirteenth birthday. At least that's what Bruno and Rudi told us. And *that* only happens every thirteen years."

Anna sank to the ground. "Oh no," she said.

Rachel looked down at her feet. "So we're stuck here for thirteen years." This time it wasn't a question.

CHAPTER 10

The sun continued to travel across the sky until it slipped behind the tall spruce trees surrounding the pillars. We loitered near the petroforms all afternoon and into the early evening, depressed and not sure what to do with ourselves. Anna and Rachel were now stretched out in the shade talking softly, while Eric napped on a backpack placed under his head.

Sutekh had left right after our failed attempt to leave, explaining that he needed to update the Chief. And as I'd watched him leave, I remembered how satisfied he had sounded when the pillars didn't work. Maybe he *knew* we couldn't leave – because he *had* tried years ago. But why wouldn't he tell us?

Then again, maybe I was just in a foul, distrustful mood.

But there must be a way to get out of here, I thought. The ancients traveled back and forth along the timeline all the time – at least that's what the scientists said – so there was no reason why we couldn't do that too. They even took the trouble to mark the wormhole locations and provide instructions ...

"That's it!" I whispered. I hurried to the nearest pillar and examined the symbols that I thought were left by native North Americans. I wasn't entirely sure, but they appeared to be different from the ones at Mit Rahina. I mean, they were obviously *slightly* different because they were created at different times and maybe by other people. But the drawings and engravings themselves were not the same, and I was sure the message was not the same either.

Anna and Rachel walked over to join me. "Did you find something, Cody?" Anna asked.

"Maybe," I said, still analyzing a section of stone. "I think we weren't able to travel back because we never read the instructions to get back."

"What do you mean?" Rachel said.

"Okay," I said, "hear me out. I think that the pillars at Mit Rahina are kind of like the departure boards at an airport. Those boards tell you when and from where your plane leaves. Right?"

The girls nodded.

"Well, we just *assumed* that we could leave this time period the same way we left our time. But that didn't work because we never checked the departure board – in this case, the pillars – for our instructions." I pointed at the stones.

Anna and Rachel looked at each other like I was talking gibberish.

So I clarified my gibberish. "We can't just walk into the Cairo airport and expect to end up in Canada. We have to read the instructions on the departure board and then go to the correct gate at a *specific* time – to end up in the right place."

"Do you have a pen or pencil?" Anna asked, catching on. "I'll sketch some of these messages and patterns so we can look at them later."

I found a pencil, but we had no blank paper, so Anna used the last page in Eric's GPS manual. Rachel and I watched as Anna skillfully copied the symbols and messages left so long ago. She was an even better artist than Rachel.

Rachel smiled for the first time in hours. "So if we can figure out the instructions left for us on these stones, maybe we can still get out of here."

"Exactly," I said. "We need to –"

I broke off when I heard people coming down the trail, from the direction of the Cree camp. It was Sutekh and the three kids we had helped that morning. The children kept their distance from the lanky adult. I didn't blame them.

Now what? I wondered.

Sutekh walked up to us and said, "The Chief has asked me to escort you back to the camp. He fears for your safety if you stay in the forest overnight." Maybe I was being paranoid again, but he said that like *he* couldn't have cared less about our safety.

I looked around the clearing. The area looked pretty harmless to me, and since I'd already spent a night in the bush, I wasn't too worried about it. Plus, we needed to figure out the meaning of those symbols as soon as possible. We had to make as much use of the fading light as we could.

I opened my mouth, about to tell Sutekh a polite variation of "buzz off and leave us alone," when one of the kids mumbled something in Cree. The boy shifted from foot to foot and looked about nervously.

"What did he say?" Anna asked.

All the talking woke Eric and he meandered over to join us. The kids gave him a sly smile and secret nod that Sutekh didn't see. I had been worried that they would rat on us, but after seeing that grin, I doubted it.

Sutekh explained their presence.

"Barks-Like-An-Otter," Sutekh pointed at the little girl who had almost died that morning, "insisted that she and her friends come with me to make sure you come back to the camp. She said you *must* return to the camp so that you will be safe from Wendigo."

"*Who*," I asked, "or *what* is that?"

"It's a silly story that the kids believe. You'll learn about him sometime."

"I don't think I want to meet him," Eric said, clearly stalling. "Look at how he's freaking out the kids."

Sutekh frowned down at Eric. "That's not what I meant. In the evenings we tell stories at the camp. There might be one about Wendigo. Don't worry. Now you have plenty of time to learn all our stories." I scowled – I didn't like what he was implying.

The children must have sensed our reluctance, because Barks-Like-An-Otter started yanking on Eric's arm, pulling him back toward camp.

Eric laughed. "Hey, Cody, I think we've made

friends for life."

Anna and Rachel looked at each other with confused expressions. I wanted to tell them about the drowning, but not in front of Sutekh. If he could keep secrets, so could we.

"A group of men from the camp has not yet returned from a trading trip down river," Sutekh said. "Some of the women have agreed to move to other tents, so that you may have a teepee to yourselves."

"Isn't the tribe worried about them? Because of that creature you warned us about?"

Sutekh shook his head. "Wendigo is a part of Cree folklore – that is all. Much like the legend of Sasquatch or the Abominable Snowman, they are stories told to frighten children." He pointed at the jittery kids with a long bony finger, as if to prove his point.

"Lots of people claim they've seen Big Foot," Eric objected to no one in particular.

"It might be nice for all of us to be together and get a proper night's sleep," Rachel said.

"And it will be dark in a few hours," Anna added.

Sutekh looked up at the sky, "We should go. It's mealtime."

"That settles it," Eric said. "If it's suppertime, let's go. I'm sick of those tasteless energy bars."

I reluctantly agreed. If there really was safety in numbers – that's what adults always said – we might be better off back at camp. And we could figure out the rest – Sutekh, the Chief, and the pillars – in comfort.

We grabbed our packs and followed Sutekh and the kids back to their campsite. Barks-Like-An-Otter skipped along beside Eric and chattered nonstop with her little pals. They made enough noise that I could stay back and tell Anna and Rachel about the drowning without fear of being overheard.

"Thank goodness that Eric was hiding in the area where they were swimming," Rachel said. "Otherwise ..."

"That explains why they were so eager to have us return to the camp," Anna said. "They wanted to return the kindness you showed them. And a way for them to do that is to keep you safe from the forest creatures – they might be mythical to us, but they are very real to them."

We knew it was dinnertime when we got to the camp because the smell of food rose to the sky like billows of smoke. As expected, Eric's gut rumbled and grumbled. A string of fresh fish was cooking over the main fire pit near the center of the camp. A lady was making some sort of bread, while a huge pot of wild rice sat steaming next to her.

We all froze and stared wide-eyed at the feast being prepared all around us. We hadn't eaten any real food for days and we were starving. The Cree ladies who were assembling supper saw us gawking and waved us over to join them. They laughed and said something to Sutekh.

Sutekh translated. "They said you should all eat as much as you can. They are joking that perhaps no one wants you back because you look half-dead."

I had to laugh too. I suppose we did look like four unhealthy kids, especially Eric and Rachel with their blond hair and lighter complexions. To the Cree, they probably looked like walking corpses.

Somehow word had spread quickly through the camp that we were back from the stones and that we weren't going anywhere. And, like magic, people poured out of teepees and gathered around the food – more food than I'd ever seen in once place. I got the feeling this was more than just their average supper – like a *welcome-to-the-family* dinner. I sure hoped not – I still planned on getting home.

Sutekh gave us each a wooden bowl and wandered away. I started off my supper with a huge scoop of wild rice. I saw a few rice husks but otherwise it looked exactly like the wild rice my mom made. And it tasted just as good. I was nervous that the meat – deer or moose or caribou – would taste gross and gamey like the stuff Uncle Mitch fed us when we visited him. But it was cooked perfectly. They didn't use – or have – as many spices as we did, but all the meats were tender and flavorful.

When we finished mopping our bowls with bannock bread, Barks-Like-An-Otter spoiled Eric and me with fresh blueberries and strawberries. Eric didn't seem to mind all the extra attention.

"It must be nice to have your own personal waitress," Rachel teased.

"I can't help it if I'm a natural hero," Eric said. "Saving people is what I was born to do – just like Indiana Jones."

I laughed and popped another strawberry in my mouth.

"If only I could remember all this," Eric continued. "I'd get an awesome grade next year in Canadian History."

"Yeah," Rachel agreed, "this is pretty amazing. We're actually spending time with the first people in Canada."

Eric scowled at the Chief over his bowl of fruit. "Too bad he smashed your camera. It would be neat to get some pictures of him and –"

"– Are you kidding?" I said. "We can't start taking pictures of the Chief with a digital camera. I mean, what would we do with the photos, anyway? We can't go back to school and do a presentation on *How I Time Traveled and Met a Real Cree Chief*."

We all laughed and then looked at Chief Raven-Feather – Sutekh had told us his name. The Chief was eating with our group, but Sutekh was farther away with another cluster of diners. I noticed the Chief's fingers had lots of small cuts on them from demonstrating to everyone how sharp his new knife was.

The Chief yelled for Sutekh to come over. He stood up without much enthusiasm, ambled over to where we were eating, and sat down with us. The Chief said something and we waited for Sutekh to translate. "The

Chief suggests you show your appreciation for the meal by presenting him with another gift."

We looked at each other in disbelief.

The Chief started laughing like a madman and slapped Sutekh on the back so hard he almost rolled over onto some leftover fish fillets.

When Sutekh recovered his composure he said, "The Chief said he is only joking with you, and that you all need to relax and not be so serious."

What a character!

After everyone had eaten their fill, all the band members pitched in and quickly cleaned up. The cooking utensils were gathered and washed on the banks of the river. And the uneaten food was carefully packaged and placed in a deep hole on the eastern edge of the camp. I suppose without a refrigerator the best way to keep stuff cool was to put it in the ground. If all that smoked meat was stored in the tents, it would definitely attract bears. They were doing everything we were taught to do in Boy Scouts, only they were never taught to do it, not like us – it was part of their culture.

We watched Sutekh help one of the ladies place a heavy stone on the cover of the food storage locker. We had a few minutes to talk before he'd be back.

"Anna has an idea – a really good idea," Rachel said.

"Oh yeah," I asked, "what is it?"

Anna turned around to make sure Sutekh wasn't coming back. "Well," she said, "what if we ignored the symbols and glyphs from all the cultures, except the ones we know are from native North Americans? Perhaps the Chief or one of the elders could make sense of those figures."

Rachel pulled out Eric's GPS manual and pointed to a specific cluster of glyphs that Anna had copied from the stones. Three small shapes formed a triangle and clearly represented the pillars – that was a no-brainer. But the other symbols were more obscure. There was a circle with a line underneath it, a crazy lightening bolt thingy, and an object I could best describe as a comb.

Eric took a quick look at it too before Rachel slipped it into her bag again. "Maybe," he suggested, "someone here can look in a Cree book and tell us what it all means."

Anna shook her head. "That's not possible. They have oral traditions."

"What does that mean?" Eric asked.

"The ancient Egyptians documented everything," Anna said. "They wrote down even the most boring day-to-day things. But the early Cree passed on all their legends and myths and ancestry through stories told orally – not through books."

Eric frowned. "But if we can't find a scribe here, how can we get your sketches translated?"

Anna nodded. "The symbols themselves still have meaning. Everything we see around camp has been adorned with symbols and patterns and artwork. To us it may only look like decoration, but I suspect the designs hold messages too."

"I still don't get it," Eric said.

Anna was patient and tried to explain. "If I took a piece of paper and painted an eye, and a heart shape, and a horseshoe, does that mean anything to you?"

"Sure," Eric said, "I see that all the time. It means, 'I ... love ... you.'"

"Exactly," Anna said. "I didn't use the English alphabet to spell that out – I used symbols – but you still understood the message. The Cree wouldn't understand my 'I love you' symbols, just as we can't understand their symbols. But still, even without a written alphabet, they are using symbols to communicate."

We all looked around the camp. Anna was absolutely right. *Everything* was decorated – the tents, the weapons, the food bowls, the clothing. I felt a new hope grow inside me. Someone – perhaps one of the elders – had to know what the symbols on the pillars meant.

The sun slipped below the horizon. One of the men threw heaps of wood onto the coals that had cooked our food. The dry logs quickly ignited and the heat pushed us back several feet. The children in the camp who had been eating their supper with their family members gathered around an old man. Older kids made a semi-circle behind the little kids, and the rest of the adults stayed back, forming a perimeter.

The Chief bellowed something to Sutekh and then pointed at us. Sutekh grimaced, but reluctantly came and sat down next to Anna. He seemed to like her more than Rachel, or Eric, or me – probably because Anna spoke Arabic too. "I am to translate," was all he said.

"Is he the storyteller?" Anna asked.

"Yes," Sutekh said. "He is our entertainer, our storyteller, and our historian. His name is Ghost-Keeper."

I felt an elbow jab me. "Now, *that's* a guy we want to talk to," Eric whispered. "If he's the historian, he has to know about their symbols – it's his job."

Rachel heard what Eric said, and she elbowed him back. "If we're going to ask for his help later, you better show some respect now."

Once the kids had settled down, he began telling stories. We couldn't understand anything Ghost-Keeper said, but it was just as entertaining to watch him. He didn't just talk, he acted out whatever he was trying to say. He stood up, he sat down, and he even leapt into the air, as spry and nimble as a cricket, provoking sharp screams from some of the kids. And me too – I jumped.

"He's terrific," Rachel said quietly.

"What is that story about?" Anna asked Sutekh, "it looks very interesting."

"He always begins with this story," Sutekh explained. "It's called *Turtles Never Run*. The children love it."

Everyone broke into laughter when his tale ended. The children implored Ghost-Keeper to continue. He pretended to be exhausted. Standing up, he faked a great yawn and suggested he was going to leave and go to sleep. But the kids wouldn't have any of that. They whined and they begged, and after a minute he sat down again with an exaggerated sigh.

The storyteller saw us grinning and waved us even closer, inviting us to be part of his audience. Ghost-Keeper said something to Sutekh, and Sutekh translated. "Next, he will tell the story *Why Beaver Has a Flat Tail*."

Sutekh nodded and the elder began again.

"Many moons ago Beaver had a long, thin tail. And his neighbor, Muskrat, had a big, fat, flat tail. Beaver loved the sound Muskrat's tail made when it hit the water."

Ghost-Keeper slapped his hands to mimic the sound of a beaver smacking his tail against the water. The sudden smacking sound made the kids, including me, jump.

"Beaver became jealous of Muskrat's beautiful tail. He thought about how much fun he could have if only he had a tail like that. He could show it to all his friends and they would be impressed with the thunderous clap it made – if only it was his."

The kids around me were all grinning. I realized that to them this was like when Eric and I laughed at a cartoon on TV, even though we'd already seen it ten times.

"Beaver couldn't eat, or sleep, or work on his dam. All he did was think about Muskrat's tail and how he wanted it. So one day he asked Muskrat if they could trade tails for one day – just one day. Muskrat said no, but Beaver wouldn't give up. Every day he pestered Muskrat to trade with him. Finally, Muskrat had enough, and he agreed to swap tails with Beaver for a day. But the following morning, when Muskrat asked for his flat tail back, Beaver shook his head."

The openmouthed children shook their heads too, voicing their disappointment with Beaver's sneaky trick.

"Muskrat screamed and begged for his tail, but Beaver ignored him and vanished into a bog. And to this day Beaver has not returned Muskrat's tail."

When Ghost-Keeper finished, I saw a lot of the adults offering satisfied nods. The stories are often different, I thought, but the message to kids is the same – be happy with what you have.

The storyteller pointed at the open space next to him. Then, he pointed at me.

Oh, no. Now what?

CHAPTER 11

Eric laughed and pushed me toward Ghost-Keeper.

I groaned inwardly and snaked my way toward the storyteller. When I was standing next to him, with my back to the fire, he said something to Sutekh.

"He asks that *you* share a story now," Sutekh explained, enjoying my discomfort. "To refuse would be an insult."

Oh brother.

Anna nodded her encouragement, and Rachel winked at me and said, "Go ahead, Cody, tell us a story."

Of course, I could have declined. I could have pretended I had a sore throat, or a stomach ache, or something. But we needed his help, and I wanted to go back home, so I took a deep breath and decided to wing it.

"This story," I began, "is called ... ahh ... *Never Believe a Fox*. Many moons ago, Handsome Fox and Hungry Fox were playing near their home. They loved their forest and their river, but as they played they began to fear that they may have to move soon because there were few mice left for them to eat. So Handsome Fox and Hungry Fox came up with a plan – they would trick the mice to come to them. They just didn't know *how* to trick the mice."

The kids laughed politely as Sutekh translated. *Maybe this wasn't so bad.*

"Handsome Fox and Hungry Fox were not very smart, so they asked Clever Fox for her advice. Clever Fox considered the problem and told Handsome Fox and Hungry Fox what to do. They left their home and went into the forest, and told all the animals that they were tired of eating seeds and wild rice and wild oats and all the things mice love. They explained that to the north – that was where Handsome Fox and Hungry Fox lived – there was so much mouse food they had to leave and go south to find fox food."

The children grinned and leaned forward, eager for me to continue. Some of the adults chatting quietly at the back stopped talking and listened to Sutekh's translations. Happy no one was falling asleep, I continued with more confidence.

"Word spread quickly among the mice that there was a land of plenty to the north – a place free of mouse-eaters and with lots of food. Handsome Fox and Hungry Fox snuck back home and waited excitedly. The mice soon followed. Their plan was working perfectly and they feasted on mice all day long. But the mice kept coming – more mice than they could eat. Handsome Fox grew monstrously fat –"

I puffed up my cheeks and pretended I had a belly like Santa Claus. Everyone laughed as Sutekh turned my story into Cree.

"– And Hungry Fox was weary of eating mice and longed for the taste of a frog or a bird. Their plan had worked too well. Finally, they had enough. They told the mice it was just a trick and that there was no extra mouse food. Word of the trick swept across the forest and reached all mice. And they all left as quickly as they came. Handsome Fox and Hungry Fox didn't have to move from their home, but they did have to work harder and harder to catch their food."

I waited for Sutekh to translate what I said and then I wrapped up my story. "So foxes are sly and sneaky and you should never trust one. The end."

Ghost-Keeper stood up – he'd been sitting on a log – and put a hand on my shoulder. He said something loudly in Cree.

Sutekh explained what the Chief said. "He will remember that story and tell it in the future. He also said that you may become his ... apprentice storyteller."

In that instant, it dawned on me that they expected us to stay with them forever – to be part of their family. *Yikes!*

I bowed politely and then quickly walked back to sit beside Eric. I didn't want to be cajoled into another tale.

"That was pretty lame," Eric said giggling.

"It wasn't lame at all, *Handsome Fox*," Rachel said.

"Huh?" Eric looked puzzled.

Rachel laughed and looked at her brother. "That story didn't sound familiar to you, *Hungry Fox*?"

"No," Eric said. "Wait. That was about us?"

Rachel shook her head.

"At least you didn't offend Ghost-Keeper." Eric indicated the storyteller with his chin. "We need to keep him on our good side."

"Yeah," I said, "maybe we can visit with him first thing in the morning."

We told Sutekh we were exhausted and excused ourselves to go to the tent assigned to us. He looked at us suspiciously, but didn't stop us. For a guy who said he'd help us, he was trying awfully hard to keep an eye on us.

Our tent was very cozy. One of the Cree ladies lit three homemade candles and placed them on the stones that formed the fire pit in the center. The candles were smelly and the smoke tickled my nose, but the flames gave the inside of the teepee a nice glow. We made ourselves comfortable on all the furs that covered the ground.

Rachel took Eric's GPS manual from her backpack and passed around the sketch Anna had made on the last page. There was just enough light to examine the glyphs.

"This sure looks a lot like what I remember seeing at the Mit Rahina pillars," I said. "But there's something different about them as well."

"Too bad the Chief had to go and smash your camera," Eric said again. He put a stack of small furs under his head to make a pillow. "You took a picture of the native North American symbols on the stones we saw in Egypt."

Rachel nodded. "It would have been nice to compare the picture of the glyphs back home with these." She pointed at the sketches Anna was now holding.

Anna stared at the page for a long time without blinking. "Wait a minute!" she cried. Anna dropped the booklet on Eric's chest, jumped up, and ran from the teepee.

"What's she up to?" I asked.

Eric shrugged. "Maybe she has to pee really badly."

I sighed and closed my eyes. I was glad we had returned to the camp. I felt safer with the Cree watching over us. With all their bush skills and survival know-how, we were definitely in *their* Sultana – on *their* turf. We continued to settle down for the night while we waited for Anna to come back.

Ten minutes later, we were starting to worry Anna had gotten lost. But then the tent flap flew open and she stormed inside, huffing and excited.

"Maybe we can still use this," Anna said. She sat down and proudly held out the small memory card from the camera. The Chief had destroyed my birthday present, but the memory stick looked intact.

"No way!" Eric said, sitting up again. "How on Earth did you find that?"

Anna grinned, pleased with her discovery. "It's dark outside, but I remembered where we had left the camera, and I looked through the broken pieces. Do you have a second camera?"

The three of us shook our heads.

"Oh," Anna said, deflated. "Does your GPS have a slot for this kind of a device?"

"Yeah, maybe," Eric said. We waited nervously for him to dig it out of the backpack. He found it, flipped it over and over, and then shook his head. "Nope."

"Too bad you guys didn't bring my electronic book reader," Rachel said. "That definitely has a memory card slot."

"Hold on," I said. "Where did you keep it? I don't remember seeing it when Eric and I left –"

"– Wait a second!" Rachel interrupted. "Is that *my* backpack?" She pointed at the bag I was holding. When I nodded, she grabbed it and ripped open a Velcro seal. A second later, with a satisfied smile, she extracted her e-book reader. Eric and I hadn't even known that pocket existed.

Rachel turned on her e-book and slid the memory card from my camera into the slot on the side. "I sure hope this works."

We gathered around the monitor and watched as Rachel flipped through the photos I had taken with my camera. Rachel paused on a picture of the scientists.

"Cody took that one in the car," Eric said, "after your dad and Rudi kidnapped ..."

"– I'm so sorry that Papa got you involved in this mess." Anna sighed. "But I'm still glad you guys came to help me out."

Rachel continued to click her way through the

pictures until she found the one from the stones at Mit Rahina.

"Stop!" I said. "That's it." She zoomed in so that the whole message filled the LCD screen.

Eric twisted the device so that he could see it better. "Cody was right. This is different than what Anna copied from the stones here. So it's true – we were trying to go back home the wrong way!"

Rachel held her piece of paper next to the e-book display. "I think the difference is in these symbols here." She tapped glyphs on the left side.

"Maybe we can work backward," Anna suggested. "Using the information we already know to be true."

"Good," Eric said, "let's try that."

"All right," I said. "So here's what we know. We traveled to this world because we were all born around the same time and during a very specific summer solstice."

Everyone nodded.

"And we know that we were able to pass through the wormhole because we stood in the center of the pillars during our thirteenth birthdays. This coincided with the cosmic alignment."

Rachel shook her head. "Right. But I'm still not sure how that helps us."

"Well – this symbol here," Eric said pointing at the screen, "has to be the symbol they used for the sun."

"Yes," Anna agreed. "See how it has rays of light shining from it."

"For sure," I said. "And these other glyphs could represent the planets that your dad talked about – the ones that line up behind the sun every thirteen years."

"Okay. So now that we know the message," Rachel said, "the symbols on the stones seem pretty logical. They've got everything included here – the pillars, the summer solstice, and the planetary alignment."

Eric poked Anna's drawing. "But what about this stuff? There are two or three symbols on the pillars, here in *this* time, that aren't on the stones back in Egypt."

"That's true," Anna agreed. "But both messages originated from the same culture – native North American – and used the same logic. So it shouldn't be too difficult to interpret their meaning."

Two of the candles in our teepee flickered and then burned out. The light was fading fast. We didn't want to start using the flashlight, so we decided to wait until the morning to decipher the rest of the symbols. Plus, we could barely keep our eyes open.

"Tomorrow," I said, "we can ask Ghost-Keeper and the other elders if they have any ideas about these figures."

Anna blew out the last candle and we all stretched out around the cold fire pit in the center of the tent. We fell asleep to the peaceful night sounds of the wilderness around us.

Only I didn't fall asleep right away.

As I listened to the wind in the trees outside and

the call of a distant loon, a thought began to trouble me. I wasn't sure what my tired brain was getting at, but it was gently trying to help me remember something – something I had seen ...

CHAPTER 12

The following morning I was roughly shaken awake.

I opened my eyes to find Barks-Like-An-Otter shoving me enthusiastically. She tugged on my arm until I sat up – my commitment to her that I wouldn't go to sleep again. I looked around the tent for the girls, but they were already gone. I rubbed my eyes and watched as Eric received the same wake-up call. She pushed and pulled on his shoulders until he too gave up. When we were both sitting upright, Barks-Like-An-Otter indicated – by pretending to shovel something in her mouth – that we should join her for breakfast.

"I suppose if I can't sleep," Eric said, "I may as well eat."

Summer-Blessing – that's Barks-Like-An-Otter's mother – was waiting for us outside the tent. She waved for us to follow her and join her and the girls for breakfast. Breakfast was fresh bannock bread with honey and mashed berries. It tasted better than any pancake I'd ever had back home.

Anna and Rachel had ripped the page with her sketch from Eric's manual and were keenly studying it. They had already eaten. Rachel took the paper, passed it to Summer-Blessing, and tapped the glyphs. Summer-Blessing said something in Cree, shook her head, and looked around the camp. She spotted Sutekh speaking with the Chief and pointed to him.

"I guess she can't help us either," I said.

Rachel stood up and took the page to an elder who was trying to patch one of the birch bark canoes. He stopped dripping pine tar on a crack and smiled at Rachel. I watched closely as the man examined the sketch and then, just like Summer-Blessing, pointed at Sutekh.

Rachel took Anna's drawing to three other Cree and got similar reactions – shrugs, head shakes, and gestures toward Sutekh.

This was getting more and more suspicious.

Rachel joined us again several minutes later. "No one knows anything," she said, passing Anna the paper.

"Hmmm," I said.

Eric put down the piece of bread he was just about to pop in his mouth. "What's up?" he asked.

"I think they know a lot," I said. "They just don't know how to tell us what they know."

"What do you mean?" Rachel asked.

I took a piece of birch bark from a nearby pile of kindling and tried to flatten it as best I could. Then with a piece of half-burnt wood from the cold fire pit, I drew one of the simplest symbols I had seen – a circle with four lines coming out from four directions.

I looked around to make sure Sutekh wasn't watching, and then I showed the sketch to Summer-Blessing. I tried to make my eyes big, like I was asking her, "Does this look familiar?"

She looked at my drawing and didn't hesitate. Her arm shot straight out and she pointed at the sun.

"Whoa!" Eric said.

"Maybe she just saw Anna's drawing," Rachel said. "And now she's guessing."

"Well that's just it," I said. "The symbol I drew with the charcoal was from the pillars back in Egypt. It's not even on the stones here, or on Anna's sketch." I tapped the paper Anna was holding.

I checked to make sure Sutekh couldn't see us. He still had his back to us, so I poked Summer-Blessing on the shoulder to get her attention. When she looked at me I traced the intricate painting design on her teepee with my finger. Then I pointed at her.

She understood what I was asking and shook her head. *No, I did not paint the teepee.*

I lifted my shoulders and made my eyes big. *Who did draw this?*

She looked around the camp and pointed at Sutekh.

"Oh!" Eric said.

"What do you mean, 'Oh'?" Anna asked.

"I think that Sutekh knows what all the symbols mean," I said, "but he doesn't want to tell us."

"But why would he not tell us what he knows?" Anna asked.

"Because he doesn't want us to leave. Maybe he's lonely and wants company," Eric suggested.

"I bet there's a lot more to it than that," I said, staring at Sutekh.

Rachel said, "Like what?"

"Or maybe," Eric rambled on, "he's afraid that if we leave, we'll rat on him. Maybe he thinks EAL will come here and haul him back ... or kill him, because he didn't live up to his end of the bargain."

"But that's not even possible," Rachel said. "We *know* no one can come here for another thirteen years, and even then, only if they were born during the solstice."

"*We* know that," Eric said, "but does Sutekh?"

Everyone was quiet for a few minutes as we considered Sutekh. He was still chatting with the Chief at the far end of the camp and I was still watching them both. "You know," I said, "it's also possible that the truth could be a little of everything."

"So what's your theory?" Eric asked.

"He probably does want to stay here," I said. "He said he's afraid of EAL, and even if we don't believe it, he believes it. And, he may actually care about the Cree — who are now his family — and maybe he doesn't want EAL to come in here and take advantage of them either."

Anna nodded. "That might be his main reason for preventing us from going home." She sounded like she felt sorry for him. "And he can't take a chance that we might ruin his perfect life."

Rachel looked over her shoulder and toward Sutekh. "But it's still not our fault if he doesn't believe us that we *don't* want to hurt him."

Eric nodded. "And it's pretty rotten of him to keep

four kids trapped here, only because he's suspicious and paranoid. EAL might be a big greedy company, but I doubt they'd come here and kill him just because he didn't come back to work."

"Let's just forget about Sutekh for now," I said, "and get back to the *real* puzzle – the symbols on those stones." I pointed at the paper Anna was holding. "We all agree that we can't trust him – for whatever reason – so let's just decipher this message and get the heck out of here."

"Yeah," Eric nodded. "We're on our own."

Anna stared fixedly at the drawing on her lap. "When Rachel showed the other Cree my drawing, they all shook their heads – like they don't know anything. So where do we start?"

"I think they shook their heads because they can't speak English," I said. "But they *all* pointed to Sutekh. And that's either because he speaks English, or because he's the artist who painted all this stuff."

"Maybe ..." Rachel said. "But could he really have learned *all* their symbols in thirteen years?"

"Hmmm ..." Anna said, contemplating the question. "It's possible. A fast learner could easily memorize the meaning of one or two hundred glyphs."

"Bits and pieces of the images we need to interpret have probably been painted on most of these teepees," I said. "If you look carefully you'll find that someone has been using similar symbols and glyphs as artwork for years."

That was what was bothering me last night. Some of the symbols on the pillars were almost identical to the decorations on the tents!

"We're getting real close to figuring this thing out," Eric mumbled, "and I bet *he's* getting nervous about it."

Our heads automatically turned toward Sutekh.

Anna took a deep breath and slowly let it out. "But if we can't ask Sutekh for his help, what are we going to do?"

"We need to *act* like nothing's wrong," Rachel said.

"Yeah," Eric agreed, "or else he might really mess up our chance of escaping from this place."

I nodded. "But at the same time we have to work quickly to figure out what those unknown symbols mean. I'd hate to find out tomorrow that whatever we're waiting for – the solstice or whatever – has already passed."

"What could it be?" Anna wondered out loud.

"Who knows," I said, looking at Anna's drawing for the hundredth time. "A meteor shower, a comet, an eclipse, a thunderstorm – heck, it could be anything."

"I just hope we haven't missed it," Eric said. "I don't mind camping here for a few days, but I sure don't want to live here forever."

"You do live here, silly," Rachel teased. "Remember, this is Sultana."

Eric snorted. "You know what I mean."

We helped Summer-Blessing clean up after breakfast, and then lent a hand with some camp chores. After we were done, we put our plan in action. It was simple: Anna would distract Sutekh by pretending to want to learn Cree, while Rachel and Eric and I quizzed the elders and Ghost-Keeper about the symbols.

Anna persuaded Sutekh to go for a walk to the stones. She told him she wanted to learn the Cree words for everything they saw along the way. Once they were on the trail and out of sight we went to work.

Rachel grabbed Anna's sketch and took off to find the Chief, and Eric and I searched for Ghost-Keeper. We found him making arrowheads behind one of the tents. He smiled at us and looked more than happy to take a break.

I had made a second charcoal sketch of the symbol that looked like a sun on some birch bark, and that's what we showed him. He seemed delighted. I realized that he probably thought I was preparing for my training as his apprentice, which made me feel slightly guilty. He said something in Cree and stared at the sky. I thought he might be saying a prayer, but then I realized he was waiting for a cloud to slide away. When the sun finally poked out again, Ghost-Keeper pointed up at it with a half-finished stone arrowhead.

"So far, so good," Eric said.

"Now let's try the other symbols." I took a blackened stick and drew one of the unknown glyphs. I could have shown him the whole series of images at once, but I was afraid it might be confusing.

Ghost-Keeper waited patiently for me to finish it. He seemed in no hurry to get back to work. When I was done he took the birch bark and examined it.

Taking his time, he scanned the horizon and the sky around us.

"What's he looking for?" I wondered.

"Well, it can't be the sun," Eric said. "It's right there." He pointed at the sun.

"And it's daytime, so he can't possibly be searching for planets, or meteors, or comets, or –"

"– What about the moon?" Eric said. "Could he be looking for that?"

"Yeah, maybe." I tried to make a circle with my hands and then pretended that circle was moving across the sky.

Ghost-Keeper nodded.

"I don't know ..." Eric said. "He could be saying 'yes' to anything – an egg, a shooting star, a bird."

The storyteller made a circle with his hands – just like I did – and then moved his hands over our heads. Except when he did it, he slowly closed and opened his hands – like a moon waxing and waning.

"Okay," Eric admitted, "*that* is definitely a moon."

I nodded to Ghost-Keeper and said, "Excellent!" He grinned in response.

Eric pointed to my drawing and then made a half-moon out of his hands.

He shook his head.

Eric made a complete full moon with his fingers and showed Ghost-Keeper.

He nodded and pointed through the trees behind us.

Eric and I turned around and saw a crisp full moon dropping between the spruce trees.

"Holy smokes!" I said.

"It's a full moon symbol," Eric cried. "And the full moon is today – right now!"

Just then, Rachel ran around the corner and came hurtling at us. "It's today!" she screamed. "The cosmic event is today!" She paused and tried to catch her breath.

Ghost-Keeper, startled by Rachel's sudden arrival, dropped the arrowhead he had been holding. He ignored the fallen stone and gave Rachel a welcoming grin. At least *he* liked kids.

"It's the full moon, right?" Eric said, looking for confirmation.

"Yes," she said. "It's the full moon, it's summertime, and it's today!"

Rachel explained that the Chief had agreed that the round symbol represented a *setting* full moon. But she also found out that the comb-thing and the squiggly-lightening-bolt-thing represented the longest day of the year.

She summarized her complete findings for us. "So what the ancients were saying is that the wormhole shortcut will open up here when the full moon sets at *the same time* as the longest day of the year."

"But that was yesterday," Eric said, "wasn't it?"

"Yesterday was definitely a solstice day," I said. "But the full moon wasn't visible during the day."

"So we still have a chance to get home," Rachel beamed.

Ghost-Keeper was still watching us with interest, but didn't say anything. I felt a twinge of regret that I couldn't stay and be his apprentice. He was a pretty cool guy.

"Yeah, it does make sense," I said, "Rudi told us that some astronomical events can last for days or even years, while others come and go quickly – like a full moon. If the setting of today's full moon occurs at the same time as the end of this year's solstice cycle, maybe we can still make it out of here."

"Well, we better make it out of here today, because we won't get a second chance tomorrow," Rachel said.

"Why not?" Eric asked, alarmed.

"The moon's complete cycle is only about a month long and it changes from day to day. And that means our window to escape will be gone by tomorrow."

"Then we need to find Anna," I said, "and get to the pillars." I pulled my wristwatch from my pocket and studied the dials. "We've got maybe about an hour before the full moon will set."

My heart was pounding so loudly I could hardly think straight. *We needed to move!*

"Let's get the backpacks," Eric said, "and head for the stones."

Suddenly we heard a commotion by the canoes.

Ghost-Keeper took a few steps and looked around a corner of the teepee. He grinned from ear to ear, and headed to the riverbank.

"Now what?" Eric asked.

The three of us followed the storyteller. A dozen Cree were lined up along the bank, yelling and waving at three approaching canoes. I saw the Chief walking toward all the action, and I don't know why, but he didn't look happy. He pushed a few teenagers out of his way and then barked orders that people seemed to ignore.

"Stop!" I hissed.

Eric froze in front of me and Rachel bumped into my back.

"Someone's coming from downriver," I said.

Rachel pushed past me so she could see. "It must be the trading party returning."

"Perfect," I said.

"Huh?" That was Rachel. "Why?"

"Duh," Eric said, "because this is a terrific diversion. Everyone will be occupied with the return of the traders down by the water, and we can slip away."

We walked to the teepee and collected our gear. We tried hard to make it look like we were *not* in a hurry as we walked away from the camp. I felt bad not saying goodbye, but we needed them to think we were just going for a walk. If the Chief suspected that we had figured out a way home, he might send his men to stop us.

When we were back in the bush and out of sight of

the camp, we started hustling.

"I sure hope Anna and Sutekh are still at the stones," Rachel said, trying to catch her breath.

I slowed down a bit too. "Don't worry," I said, trying to sound confident. "We're *all* going home together."

Rachel traded her lighter backpack for Eric's heavier one and carried it for a while as we jogged toward the pillars. My heart wasn't just beating fast because of the quick pace. There was still a chance we hadn't interpreted the symbols correctly. Or we had missed whatever astrological anomaly was supposed to send us home.

The thought of never seeing Sultana again – my Sultana – was unbearable. I already missed my parents, and my bed, and spying on Dr. Murray, and ... and everything, really. We had to find Anna and we had to get home. The feeling of panic and my desire to leave gave me a fresh burst of energy. I picked up my tired feet and continued running toward the ancient pillars.

"We're here!" Eric blurted. He kept jogging until he was at the center of the stones.

Rachel and I followed him and threw our packs on the ground. I searched for the moon and found it. The whole thing was still visible above the horizon, between the trees. But it was sinking fast.

We don't have much time, I thought.

"Rats!" Rachel said. "They're not here!"

Anna hadn't been on the path here, so if she was anywhere, she'd be here. But she wasn't.

"ANNA!" Eric screamed.

I cupped my hands around my mouth and joined him. "ANNA! IT'S TIME TO GO!"

Silence.

I looked at the moon. I was sure it had dropped a few more degrees.

"What should we do?" Rachel asked.

Panic was taking a firm hold of me now.

"We're not leaving without her."

"I know *that*," she said, "but we have to figure something out."

"Hey, there's Sutekh," Eric said, pointing toward the south.

I searched for a glimpse of a smaller figure next to him – but he was alone.

We rushed to meet him as he walked toward us.

"Where is she?" I asked, nearly shouting. We didn't have time for polite small talk – we had to find Anna.

He didn't even bother asking us why we were back at the stones. "She is at the camp," Sutekh said. The scarab tattoo on his neck pulsed and twitched. A smile spread across his face and beads of sweat popped out on his forehead.

"Why?" Eric challenged. "I thought she was coming with you here?"

Sutekh flinched. "We were on our way here, but then we heard the yelling announcing the return of the traders. So we walked back together."

"Why did you come back here then?" I asked.

"I ... I wanted to fetch you back," Sutekh's eyes

darted all over like he was watching a ping-pong game. "Come, let's go to camp. There will be a feast and many presents from the traders."

"I don't believe you," Rachel snapped. "You're a liar."

I glanced behind me and my heart sank. The moon was now almost touching the horizon. We only had a few minutes left to make a decision – leave without Anna, or find Anna.

Sutekh wiped his sweaty face and tried to compose himself. "Please. It's important that we leave this place. The Chief won't be happy you have returned here." He seemed desperate to get us away from the stones.

"Sure, sure," Rachel said. "*You* are the only one who doesn't want us near the pillars."

This was nuts! We didn't have time for a stupid debate.

And then I had an idea.

I glared at Eric to get his attention. He caught my eye and I angled my head toward Rachel's backpack.

"Okay," I said, trying hard to sound friendly. "We'll go back with you. We only wanted to take another look at the stones. That's all."

I hoped I knew what I was doing.

CHAPTER 13

Sutekh gave us a smile that I knew was phony.

I whispered in Rachel's ear, "Count to thirty and have a tantrum." I pretended to help her with her backpack while I unzipped the outside pocket and pulled out the zapper.

"Okay, Sutekh," I said, "lead the way."

He paused, gave me a suspicious look, and said, "No, I would like *you* to guide us back."

Oh, oh! I think he's on to me.

I obediently headed off toward camp, but before I'd even taken ten steps, I heard Rachel yell, "I'M NOT GOING ANYWHERE!"

I whirled around.

Sutekh turned and stared at Rachel.

"You don't have a choice." Sutekh retorted. He walked threateningly toward Rachel and reached out to grab her shoulders. But I was ready.

I pushed the zapper into the back of his neck and pressed the button.

ZAP!

Sutekh convulsed violently and fell to the earth. His eyes closed slowly until he looked like he was asleep. At least for a few minutes.

"Nice work," Eric cheered. "But next time I want a

turn using that thing."

"This is horrible!" Rachel said. "There's no way we'll have time to go back to camp and get Anna."

"Forget about the camp," I said, searching for the moon between the spruce trees. "Anna's around here somewhere. And we have about five minutes to find her before he wakes up, and before the moon disappears."

"How do you know that?" Rachel asked.

"Sutekh and Anna might have heard the shouts when the Cree saw the canoes coming, but there's no way we could have missed them on the trail. She must be nearby."

"I get it," Rachel said. "He knew we figured out a way home, and didn't want *any* of us to make it out of here."

"Okay, let's spread out," I suggested, "and see if we can find her. And hurry!"

We fanned out into the forest around the pillars. I heard Eric scream her name in the distance, and I did the same. "ANNA!"

We *had* to bring her home. It wouldn't be right to leave her behind. But if we didn't find her ... could we risk staying behind?

"ANNA!" I heard Rachel yell. "WHERE ARE YOU?"

We were running out of time.

KA-KAWWW! A raven called out somewhere ahead of me.

Come on, Anna, where are you?

The stupid raven cried out again. *KA-KAWWW!*

Was that a warning call? Was it trying to tell me something? I tore through the forest in the direction of the eerie bird noise. Branches scratched at my face and arms as I bolted toward the raven.

Anna! I stopped dead in my tracks. She was lying behind a fallen tree. Her arms and legs were bound with a short length of homemade rope and she had a leather gag in her mouth.

"SHE'S OVER HERE!" I bellowed.

I gently pulled the gag from her mouth. She was shaking, but still managed to talk. "I was so worried you would leave without me," she whispered. "I thought I would be stuck here, with *him*, forever."

"We wouldn't leave without you, Anna," I assured her.

Eric crashed through the trees. He froze when he saw Anna, but then moved to help me untie the rope around her arms and legs. Together we helped her to her feet and got her moving back to the pillars. Rachel met us halfway. "He's gone," she said.

"Who's gone?" I asked, dreading the only answer she could give us.

"Sutekh – he's gone." Rachel tried to catch her breath. "I cut across the stones to get here, and he wasn't where we left him."

"He might've returned to camp ..." Eric said. "Where who knows what he'll tell the Chief."

"We have to get into that wormhole before they come back," I said.

We stuck to the original plan to send Anna and Rachel through first. Rachel kept an arm around the still-shaky Anna to steady her, while Eric and I waited for the shortcut to the future to open up. "He knew we were going to try and leave today," Anna said, sounding almost like herself again. "He didn't want us to go – any of us. I think he may have gone crazy here over the years."

"Yeah," Rachel said, "we know. But it's going to be okay now. We'll be home soon."

"Here we go again," Eric said, pacing around the girls.

The four of us faced the setting full moon. It seemed to grow bigger in size as it traveled toward the horizon. I knew it was just an optical illusion, but I swear it was twice as big as it usually was.

Another minute passed.

"Please work this time," Rachel mumbled. "Please take us home."

Thirty more seconds.

"Did you hear that?" Eric asked.

"Shhh," Rachel hissed.

This time we all heard it. It started like it did in Egypt, when Rachel vanished – with the faint sounds of electricity. First a few quiet static snaps, like wires touching a car battery, and then louder charges, like from a lightning strike ...

And then they were gone. It was like someone took a movie screen and pushed the top and bottom together, while a movie was still playing. The girls collapsed into a single point of light and then vanished.

Eric pumped his fist into the air. "Excellent!"

"Thank goodness," I said, "Now it's our turn."

But before I could step into the center, where Anna and Rachel had been, two powerful arms yanked me backward. I spun around and stared up into the face of a furious-looking Sutekh.

I glanced beside me for Eric, but he had his own problems. Two young warriors had a hold of his arms and he wasn't going anywhere either.

"Let me go!" I yelled at him. "We want to leave!"

"The Chief will decide your fate," he snarled. For the first time, I felt frightened. Spittle had built up at the corners of Sutekh's mouth like foam and I realized Anna was right – he was crazy.

"That'll take too long, you idiot!" Eric screamed. "Let go of us right now. Or I'll tell EAL ... and ... and everyone else where you are."

Sutekh laughed. "You won't tell anyone anything, because you'll never go home again."

Suddenly we heard a mob of people coming from the direction of the camp. First the pounding of feet reached us, followed by excited talking. The Chief and what looked like the rest of the camp had followed us to the pillars. Most of the Cree stayed away from the triangle formed by the three stones. But the Chief and several men walked right up to us.

Sutekh had a smug look on his face. "For years I

prayed that no one would find me – that the secret of the stones would remain a mystery," he said. "Rachel's arrival here caused me great concern. But I thought that was an accident, and that EAL would not send others ..."

"No one *sent* us, you dummy," Eric said. "We told you, we're only here to bring the girls back. And anyway, why would they send *kids*?"

"Don't try to trick me!" Sutekh screamed. "I know EAL sent you, and now more will follow. You have ruined everything for these people – my people – and you must be punished."

That didn't sound good at all.

A large Cree man we didn't recognize stepped forward and spoke to the Chief. He must have been away on one of the hunting parties. He had twice as many bear claws and decorations adorning his body as the Chief. I blinked and realized *this* was the real Chief. Raven-Feather might have been a backup chief, or an assistant chief, but this guy was the actual Chief.

Barks-Like-An-Otter pushed her way through the small crowd and ran to the large man. He scooped her up with one powerful arm and hugged her close. Barks-Like-An-Otter pointed a finger at Eric and then at me and started jabbering in Cree. The man's eyes widened and he gave her a tight hug before he set her down on the grass again.

Sutekh began sweating like crazy and tried to get the attention of the men near him. But before he could finish whatever he wanted to say, the Chief shouted at the men holding Eric.

They immediately let go of his wrists and backed off.

Sutekh started to whine, but the Chief pushed him away from me. Then, the Chief grabbed both of my shoulders and held me at arm's length. He stared at me for a few seconds, yanked me close, and gave me a bear hug that squeezed the air from my lungs.

Sutekh continued complaining in Cree, but no one paid him any attention.

The Chief pointed at Barks-Like-An-Otter – I realized she must be his daughter – and bobbed his head repeatedly, while mumbling in Cree. I had no idea what he was saying, but it seemed like he was thanking me. He took three giant strides backward and indicated with his hands that we were free to leave through the stones if we wanted to.

Yes, we wanted to.

I was ecstatic! I could have given everyone there – except Sutekh, of course – a hug. I was *that* relieved. But we didn't have a second to spare. We needed to dive into that wormhole before it slammed shut again. I nodded my thanks to the Chief, gave everyone a quick goodbye wave, and joined Eric in the center of the pillars.

I glanced at the sky but couldn't see the moon anywhere.

"Where the heck is it?" Eric shouted. He couldn't see it either.

My legs threatened to collapse under me. *Were we too late?* I felt like throwing up.

"Wait!" I heard Eric say. "What ..."

I turned to face him, but he had already started to vanish. Something pulled and twisted at my body and then I spiraled down a void until I either blacked out or fell asleep – I'm not really sure which.

"Cody!" a voice said.

"Come on, wake up." A different voice now, with a pleasant German accent. "I think I hear the police."

Here we go again, I thought.

"Hey, man, we made it!" Definitely Eric. I turned my head away and groaned. "We're back in Egypt."

"What's the problem then?" I mumbled.

I opened my eyes. I sensed that Eric, Rachel, and Anna were nearby, but it was nighttime and my eyes still hadn't adjusted. The stars shone brightly overhead and warm sand pressed against my back.

"The problem is that there's lots of noise coming from the parking lot," Rachel said, her face coming into focus. "We need to hide."

I sat up slowly, trying to get my bearings again. I ignored the sound of a distant police siren and looked around quickly. Pillars, sand, ruins, stone – excellent! I smiled. We were back at Mit Rahina. "Let's move," I said.

Eric helped me up and guided me deeper into the open-air museum. The four of us wound our way through the jumble of columns and toppled boulders.

We settled in to hide behind a stone wall, just as two flashlight beams lit up the sky near the pillars, where we had all been minutes earlier. The powerful lights sliced across the sky and cut through the night. I held my breath and waited.

What a shame it would be to get caught by the police now, after everything we'd been through.

The flashlights and short shouts left the area five minutes later, but still we waited in silence for another half hour. We had learned in our adventures to be patient and cautious – okay, maybe 'paranoid' was a better word for it. Finally Eric let out a "Whew," which startled all of us, and dug out the satellite phone. It was late at night in Egypt, but the stars and a big moon made it easy to see what we were doing.

"The wormhole made a tremendous noise when we arrived," Anna whispered, indicating the stones with a twist of her head. "I think someone must have called the police."

"It's a good thing we hid," I said, taking the phone from Eric. I turned it on and waited for the satellites to find our phone. Rudi said they had programmed his cell number into the speed dial memory, so all I had to do was press two buttons and wait.

After the third ring I heard an excited Bruno say, "Hello."

"We're back!" I said.

There was a long pause and I thought I'd lost the connection. But then I heard him say, "Are you *all* back?

Did the police see you?"

"Yes." I shook my head. "I mean, *yes* we're all safe – Anna's with us. And *no* the police didn't see us."

He was starting to blubber. I could barely understand him as he tried to explain that the police had just left the parking lot again. Apparently he had been waiting there with Rudi and Aubey since the day we disappeared. "It's safe now," he said. "Please hurry –"

His voice suddenly trailed off. I knew he was still on the line – I could hear the crunch of car tires on gravel and the slamming of car doors. But he wasn't saying anything.

"Hello?" I said. "Bruno? Are you still there?"

My friends leaned in close, trying to hear what was happening on the other end of the line.

"What the heck's going on?" Eric whispered.

"Shhh," Rachel hissed.

Several minutes later Bruno spoke again. "Cody?" He said my name so calmly, it made the hairs on the back of my neck stand up. He was freaking me out.

"Yeah," I said, "is everything okay?"

He seemed to ignore me. "The police contacted EAL, and they are now here in the parking lot. They will be asking you all a few questions when you get here. I assured them you *didn't* travel anywhere, but they'd like to hear it from you. Do you understand?"

I nodded slowly and then realized he couldn't see me. I said, "Yeah," and turned the phone off. *Now what?*

Anna spoke first. "What's wrong?" Her voice

quivered slightly.

I quickly explained what Anna's dad said. "So I think we better get our stories straight. If they're smart they'll split us up to see if we say the same thing."

"Why can't we just tell them what really happened?" Eric said. "We'll be famous."

Rachel shook her head. "Are you crazy? Remember what Bruno and Sutekh said – EAL is greedy. If that's true, they only want to use the stones to get rich, and they'll take advantage of all those ancient cultures."

"But Sutekh was a lunatic – we need to tell someone about him," Eric countered. "And Bruno doesn't know that for sure."

"We can't take that chance," I said. "We *can't* tell them what really happened."

I saw Anna nod under the moonlight. "Sutekh wasn't good, but we have to protect him and the Cree, and say *nothing* happened."

"We vanished in the wormhole," I said, looking at Eric, "bounced around for who-knows-how-long, and then reappeared back at the stones. Let's keep it super simple or they might trip us up in our lie."

"Okay, let's get this over with," he said reluctantly. "And then let's see if we can find an all-night pizza place. I'm starving."

We bumped our way through the ruins and back to the main trail. I wasn't sure what to expect from our impending meeting with EAL, and I was pretty anxious. Anna seemed less concerned and picked up the pace when we hit the wide gravel path that lead to her dad and uncle. We spilled into the parking lot and were greeted enthusiastically by Aubey and the scientists.

I scanned the area. Fifty feet away a shiny black limo sat under one of the street lights. A huge man – probably the driver – stood guard next to the vehicle while a smaller man paced tight circles beside the car.

Anna ignored the strangers and pounced into the open arms of her dad with such force, she almost knocked him to the ground. Rudi sandwiched her in Bruno's arms and she disappeared, wedged between the two brothers.

Aubey welcomed Eric and me with awkward handshakes. "Good work, boys," he said. "Very good work."

"It's good to see you too," Eric said, thumping Aubey on the back.

When Aubey saw Rachel he stopped pumping my arm. He lifted her right off the ground, squeezed her close, and said, "I'm glad you're safe."

Rachel squealed and he set her back down on the gravel. "It's nice to be back," she said with a laugh.

"Listen," Aubey suddenly whispered. "That man behind me is Mr. Rahotep. He is with Egyptian Antiquities Limited. Just be respectful and do as he says."

The three of us nodded.

"ENOUGH!" Mr. Rahotep screamed. His sharp

voice cut through the quiet night. I guess he got tired of watching our friendly reunion.

Anna broke away from her dad and uncle and joined Eric and Rachel and me. We had made it this far as a team, and we would end this crazy journey together. The four of us stood side by side, forming what I hoped looked like an imposing sight. Aubey and the brothers were ten feet behind us.

I nudged Eric gently with my elbow. "Remember," I said, "we want to keep our story simple."

Mr. Rahotep walked over to us with short brisk strides. He was wearing traditional Egyptian clothes, and seemed to have a no-nonsense demeanor. His white robes flapped all over the place as he stormed our way. When he was four feet away, he stopped and studied each of us for several seconds.

Please don't pick me. Please don't pick me.

His arm shot out and he pointed right at my face.

Rats!

"You," he said.

I gulped. "Me what?"

"Follow me." Mr. Rahotep spun around and headed back to his limo.

I looked at my friends, shrugged my shoulders, and followed him.

When we were near his car again, he turned and said, "Tell me what happened at the pillars." He paused to give me a prolonged stare. "Tell me *everything*."

I tried to swallow some spit so that I could talk.

"We fell into blackness," I began. "I spun around and around for a long time. It was very scary. Then suddenly I woke up here again." Mr. Rahotep's dark eyes darkened even more. I gulped. This guy was intense. "And that's all I remember," I added.

"Are you saying that you didn't go *anywhere*?" Mr. Rahotep asked.

"No, I went to those stupid stones." I pointed at the open-air museum.

He shook his head, frustrated. "I *meant*," he said slowly, "did you go anywhere *after* you disappeared?"

"Is *nothing* a place?" I asked. "Because that's all there was – lots of nothing. If you close your eyes right now, you'll be in the same place where I was. It's just blackness and spinning – horrible, really."

Mr. Rahotep took a deep breath and let it our slowly. "So you didn't find anything, see anything, or meet anyone after you vanished?"

I continued with my dumb-guy act. "Well, no. Who would I meet in *nothingland*? I didn't even see my friends there. It was just black."

He gave me a painfully long, unblinking stare, and then said, "And if I asked your friends – what would they say?" His eyebrows rose way up on his forehead.

That sounded to me like it could be a trick question, but I didn't have time to consider many possible answers. "You can ask them," I said, trying to sound like I didn't care if he did or didn't. "But the exact same thing happened to all of us."

Mr. Rahotep straightened his small figure. "I see." He seemed to be considering his options. "I think we are done here." He nodded at his driver, who sprang to life and opened the door for his master. Before he climbed into his car, Mr. Rahotep turned to give me a final threatening look. "I will be keeping an eye on you and your friends. You can be sure of that."

I watched as the car slipped away into the night.

Rachel stared through the lens of my new camera and positioned us in the center of the frame. It reminded me of our last few days in Egypt. I had thought Mr. Rahotep would for sure kick us out of the country, but we weren't let off the hook that easily. Before we returned home, we visited museums and pyramids, and even had a ride down the Nile. Since Bruno and Rudi made us delete all the photos of the pillars, now we only had photos from the second part of our vacation.

Still, in spite of the way the whole trip started – with our kidnapping, and Anna and Rachel disappearing – I didn't regret any of it. We couldn't tell a soul back home about the stones, or the wormhole, or our trip to the past, but it was something we'd never forget.

"Jeepers!" Eric yelled, pulling me back from my thoughts – back to *our* Sultana. "Just take the picture."

"Then stand closer to the pillar," Rachel ordered,

"so I can get both of you in the same photo."

I had promised Anna I would e-mail her a photo of our pillars in Sultana as soon as we made it home. We had unpacked the day before and said our final goodbyes to Aubey, and now we were getting ready to cut the grass again in the cemetery. You wouldn't believe how much grass can grow in a week.

Rachel waited for us to get in position. "You know," she said, looking around. "I'm happy to be back in our Sultana, but if we *had* to stay with the Cree forever, it wouldn't have been so bad."

I nodded. "You're right about that." I had been thinking the same thing for days. The Cree were super-friendly, they liked to laugh and tell stories, and they took good care of each other. Sure, we had visited them hundreds of years in the past, but in a lot of ways they were just like us, and they had fun even without computers and other modern stuff. "I could have been Ghost-Keeper's assistant storyteller," I added.

Eric leaned on the pillar and laughed. "Heck, if they had TVs and pizza, I wouldn't have bothered coming back with you guys."

Rachel laughed as she snapped a few pictures of us leaning against a pillar.

"Wouldn't it be neat to go back and visit them some time?" I said, running my finger over the symbol some native North American made ages ago.

"Well," Eric said, "that shouldn't be a problem. We know the secret now to go back and visit the Cree.

We just have to wait thirteen years and stand in the right spot."

Rachel stomped toward us and handed my camera back. "Are you nuts? Don't you remember what Mr. Rahotep told Cody? If he ever finds out we really did time travel, or that we went back again ... well, I don't even want to think about what could happen."

"We know, we know," Eric said. "We only meant it *would* be neat to visit them again – like for a holiday. We weren't serious."

Rachel looked between her brother and me with doubt. "Sure, sure."

It would be cool to see the Cree again, but it was nice to be home too: Sultana in the twenty-first century. Now we just had to make it through the rest of our summer break without getting into any more trouble.

Fat chance.

The ARCHAEOLOJESTERS

BOOK **3**

TROUBLE AT IMPACT LAKE

Cody, Eric, and Rachel – AKA the Archaeolojesters – have returned from their time traveling adventures in Egypt. Now it's back to Manitoba and their boring old routine – or so they think! While getting ready for yet another day of fishing, Cody and Eric run into some divers who say they are recovering a sunken military plane from an old World War II base at Impact Lake. Something about their story seems off, and the kids can't resist doing some investigation. But will these clever sleuths dig up more danger than they can handle?

Join the
Archaeolojesters
on their next adventure
in Spring 2011

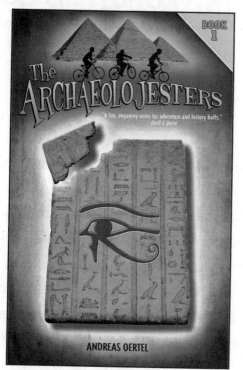

About the Author

Andreas Oertel was born in Germany and has spent most of his life in Manitoba, Canada. Fascinated by archaeology, ancient civilizations, and discovery, he can often be found exploring the local beaches with his trusty metal detector. In addition to creating "**The Archaeolojesters**" series, Andreas is also the author of the young adult novel *Deep Trouble* (Write Words Inc., 2008). He lives in Lac du Bonnet, Manitoba.

Q&A with Andreas Oertel

What inspired you to write stories that focus on history and archaeology?

I enjoy the mystery aspect of archaeology. The idea of finding something – anything at all – in the ground that may be thousands of years old is extremely cool. I love imagining where something might have come from, who might have made it, and who held it last. In archaeology every find is a mystery.

How did you learn about Cree culture?

I read constantly and the Internet is also an invaluable tool for conducting any research. But Manitoba – and much of central North America – also has a rich Cree history and it's hard to grow up around here and not have an interest in the culture. I lived in northern Manitoba for ten years and worked in remote First Nations and Métis communities. The people I met on my travels were always friendly and eager to answer any questions I had regarding their culture, history, or unique art. I was given an amazing framed birch bark biting as a gift when I left the North, and it always grabs people's attention when they see it.

If you could travel in time, where would you go?

My first choice would be ancient Egypt, around 2000 B.C. But other fun trips would include hanging out with the early North American Cree, seeing China during the Ming Dynasty, sailing the ocean with Columbus, or even sneaking on Apollo 11 and going to the moon with the first astronauts. If time travel is a possibility, any imaginable adventure is a possibility too.